MAN OF TWO WORLDS

Walter Cardish was a very ordinary, somewhat downtrodden individual. But, following an incredible accident, he recovers in hospital and finds that he has been granted the power of seeing into the future. Assuming the identity of 'The Great Volta: Prognosticator' he amasses a fortune, and a reputation as a seer. But his activities also create enemies, and soon one of them tries to kill him, and the implacable workings of his strange destiny close in upon him inexorably . . .

JOHN RUSSELL FEARN

MAN OF
TWO WORLDS

Complete and Unabridged

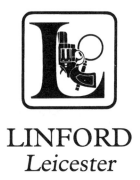

LINFORD
Leicester

First published in Great Britain

First Linford Edition
published 2009

British Library CIP Data

Fearn, John Russell, *1908 – 1960.*
    Man of two worlds
    1. Suspense fiction. 2. Large type books.
    I. Title
    823.9'12–dc22

    ISBN 978–1–84782–712–8

Published by
F. A. Thorpe (Publishing)
Anstey, Leicestershire

Set by Words & Graphics Ltd.
Anstey, Leicestershire
Printed and bound in Great Britain by
T. J. International Ltd., Padstow, Cornwall

This book is printed on acid-free paper

1

For Walter Cardish, normally a gent's wear salesman in one of London's biggest stores, it was a vast relief to be alone for once. In his business life he was perpetually under the orders of the department manager; in his private life he was perpetually under the orders of his wife Bertha — or else Tommy. Tommy was his son, nearing fourteen, with all the necessary qualifications for becoming a juvenile delinquent.

Yes, it was good to be alone. The hill scenery was somewhat dimmed by an approaching thunderstorm, the air was as still as death, and even the scent of grass and wild flower was smothered under a distinct smell of sulphur as the storm neared flashpoint — but it was good to be alone just the same.

Just here, in the Lake District, it was such a long way from London too — far enough away to forget what the grey old busy city looked like. At the moment Walter Cardish was walking across Copper's Brow — a great desolate stretch sandwiched between Rydal Water and Endor's Tarn — which meant that the hotel where he had left Bertha and Tommy for the time being was some five miles away. They had seen that a storm was gathering and refused to venture forth. Cardish, not brave in many things, had nonetheless decided to take his chance if only to enjoy the solitude of his own company and the beauty of the landscape.

Now he was not so sure of himself. The storm showed every prospect of developing into a 'stinker' when it did break. To the north and east the sky was violet, the hills mounted in indigo array against it. To the southwest the sun was glimmering like a brass tray seen by firelight. The August day had started well and was apparently going to end badly.

Conscious of a strange, inexplicable sense of danger, Walter Cardish began to increase his pace. In the far distance he had observed a crofter's hut — it might at least be shelter if he could reach it before the storm broke in earnest. He kept his eye on it, giving only an occasional glance at the ominous sky.

The faster he hurried the harder he breathed. Life in the city, and such an unhealthy one in a basement too, had not moulded him into an athlete. Indeed he was exactly the opposite — small-built, narrow-shouldered, thin-faced, with a perpetual air of expectancy about him. As indeed there was. He was always ready to spring to attention at a command, whether it came from his boss, his wife, or his son. Poor Walter Cardish! How like so many other millions of men, yet like any normal human being he had his secret ambitions, his loves and his hates, even though he never dared to confess to any of them except to himself.

Then the storm blasted forth. No other expression fits it. It did not 'break' like any self-respecting thunderstorm with several preliminary distant rumbles and a distant flash or two, to show it was warming up. Instead the overture was a savage flash of brilliant violet streamers that seemed as though they had ripped open earth and hell itself.

Cardish came to a standstill, his heart racing. His limbs were tingling, too. That appalling flash had been dangerously close to him and he was more than sure that it had left behind a distinct crater in the rockery. The air reeked of electrical discharge. From walking rapidly he changed to a run, his ears still singing from the impact of the thunder.

Then came the second flash, and this time Cardish was just in the right place to receive it. He was streaking over bare rockery towards the crofter's hut and the shimmering electrical blaze enveloped him from head to toe. He was flung a dozen feet and crashed senseless amidst the boulders. Thunder cannonaded, but he did not hear it. Rain descended in a volume reminiscent of the Deluge. Out of the absolute stillness a whistling gale rose to a shrieking hurricane. Over the Lake District there burst the worst storm in living memory and it raged for nearly six hours. What the lightning missed the hurricane destroyed, and where both

4

these elemental forces failed the flood took toll. The storm began at four-thirty in the afternoon and it was ten-thirty before a blazing golden shaft of sunlight deep behind the hills broke through the rolling, exhausted clouds. The storm was on its way elsewhere.

Or was it? That was the peculiar thing. Nobody else had the storm. The rest of the country had perfect summer weather. And it is most unusual for a storm to nearly destroy one place and then evaporate. Usually it moves in a circle and those in the track know when to start hiding the knives and covering the mirrors.

No, in this case it was just the Lake District with the hapless Walter Cardish as the apparent epicentre of the disturbance. His wife and Tommy, marooned by flood waters in the hotel, gave all the necessary details to the rescuers in rowing boats who came to their aid in the flamboyant, angry sunset. Trained guides set off, first in boats and then on foot as they came to higher ground, and so towards one in the morning they found Walter, still alive but unconscious, soaked to the skin and muttering something incoherent to himself.

He was promptly transferred to the Windermere General Hospital and here he lay in something like a coma. His wife, informed of the situation, declared that it was just about the dam' fool thing he would do and promptly sailed through the night, the yawning Tommy at her side in the first relief boat heading Windermere way.

The rest of the country, untouched by Nature's outburst, heard the news in some surprise over the radio and television.

'The Lake District,' one announcer stated, 'has been hit by a storm of unparalleled violence, lasting some six hours. In that time whole villages have been swept away, bridges torn down, buildings shattered by lightning bolts, and hundreds of people rendered homeless or been killed and injured by lightning. The full extent of the damage is not yet known due to the difficulty in getting news from the flooded areas. Elsewhere in Britain it has been a bright, sunny day, and the weather forecast indicates that these conditions will continue. The meteorologists are unable to account for the Lake District disaster. Their charts show the area to be under the influence of the anticyclone which is dominating the rest of the country.'

So said the weather forecasters, and for some days afterwards scientists were also at work examining the problem. They had little data to go upon, however. The records of the Lake District weather station simply showed the amount of rain that had fallen, the peak wind velocity, and the maximum-minimum temperatures. In short, no more than would normally be recorded in any storm. Nor did interviews with the stricken ones offer much information. Lurid tales of savage lightning flashes and hurricane winds were sensational but not scientific . . . So at length, during which time Walter Cardish still lay in hospital, the business was put down to a freak of Nature and that was that.

Certain scientists, however, knew that

the Lake District affair was not a freak of Nature. Those scientists were big-headed, slow-moving beings with superb minds and no consciences whatever. The scientists of Mazor in fact, ruling faction of their mighty race, who regarded the strange storm on Earth as the final outburst of one of their experiments.

'It would appear,' observed the First Mathematician of Mazor, 'that our new dimensional portal is to some extent quite successful though unfortunately undisciplined. The equational vibrations we built up got out of hand and travelled not only back into our parallel world, where they created havoc, but outwards into other dimensional space, transposing certain parts of the Earth's satellite where they were finally expended.'

'And judging from the radio and television reports reaching us from our Earth satellite monitors, the inhabitants are not at all pleased about it,' another of the Mazorian scientists commented. 'They experienced what they think was a violent thunderstorm. Naturally it is beyond their small intelligences to realise that what really took place was a reshuffling of the atmospheric and electrical values of their planet in an area exactly bounded by the outflowing wave from our dimensional portal.'

The Mazorians nodded gravely and came their nearest to smiling at each other. The destruction of lives and property on another world did not matter to them in the least. They were satisfied that their latest scientific pet machine had possibilities if further developed.

'What,' asked the chief electronic expert, 'do you propose to do next?'

The First Mathematician reflected. 'Develop the portal still further, I fancy, and make it more disciplined. We require it to exert its influence for our benefit, not generate a wave which destroys and introverts matter and elements for no sensible reason — However, despite the mad behaviour of the mechanism on this first occasion, I suppose we should feel compensated by the fact that it has accidentally brought an Earthman to us. It will be interesting to study him.'

'A very low form of life,' commented

the First in Biology, with supreme contempt. 'At the moment he hardly seems able to speak coherently.'

'Still recovering from shock, I imagine,' said the First in Mentality. 'We must remember that he was suddenly transported as a pure equation from his own world to ours — hurled through a dimensional vortice before the machine's influence left him and he thereby reverted to his original matter formation, albeit with his vibrational rate attuned to our own.'

'Which seems to suggest that he must have been at the exact centre of the outflowing mathematical wave and was caught up in it,' the First in Mathematics observed, thinking. 'A most peculiar freak of electronics. We might do worse than see if this Earth creature has recovered his intelligence far enough to converse with us.'

The First in Mathematics pressed a button on the big table at which he and the ruling faction were seated. He uttered a few words in his own language into a concealed microphone and then sat back to wait.

Presently the bronze-tinted door of the chamber slid aside and two Mazorians entered, supporting between them an obviously debilitated Earthman dressed in Mazorian raiment far too big for him. And no wonder, for the Mazorians were at least seven feet tall. Between the giant guards the small, tottering figure of Walter Cardish looked positively ridiculous.

Walter Cardish? The Earthman looked exactly like him to the smallest detail. The only difference seemed to be that this Walter Cardish had a peculiarly translucent quality as though it were almost possible to see into him. His skin was strangely glasslike in its transparency. But he was Walter Cardish. No doubt of it — even though at this identical moment he was lying in a coma in a hospital in Windermere.

'Seat him,' the First in Mathematics ordered briefly, and the two guards did as instructed. Cardish was heaved to a nearby heavily ornamented chair, placed upon it, and left there. He breathed heavily, his head hanging. The Mazorians looked at one another.

'It is most instructive to see an Earth being face to face,' the biologist commented. 'Most fragile creatures, apparently.'

The First in Mathematics leaned forward. 'Earthman, do you understand what I am saying? I am using your own language. Do you understand me?'

Walter Cardish raised his head slowly. He did not look at the mathematician: instead he seemed to be trying to concentrate on something far away.

'I am talking to you,' the mathematician repeated, no trace of impatience in his voice. 'Answer me if you understand.'

In the Windermere General Hospital Walter Cardish moved uneasily.

'Yes,' he whispered. 'Yes, I can hear you — and I understand you.'

'About time,' his wife commented shortly, and gave a glance at the white-coated surgeon standing nearby.

'Try and concentrate on what I am saying, Mr. Cardish,' he said. 'You must break this coma that is upon you. There is no logical reason for it. You haven't sustained any injuries to your brain and you recovered many days ago from the exposure and shock you suffered during the storm. You understand?'

'Yes — ' Cardish stirred slowly and opened his eyes.

He gazed dully at the surgeon, then at his wife. She tightened her lips and waited.

'For heavens' sake, Walter, how much longer?' she demanded. 'For four days now you've been lying there muttering to yourself and keeping your eyes closed. All the experts here say you're all right, and I agree with them. Wake up, can't you?'

Cardish kept looking at her and there was such a queer light in his eyes she felt uncomfortable. But it was a definite fact that from that moment Cardish began to improve. In two more days he was pronounced fit to leave the hospital, well enough physically but still slightly 'queer' mentally. Since most of Lakeland had been washed out there was nothing for it but to return to London. Yes, to London — and to work, and Bertha and Tommy for another weary year.

'Why,' Bertha demanded, when they were in the train bound for home, 'do you have to keep looking so barmy, Walter?'

'Like you'd been hit with a brick,' Tommy explained helpfully.

'I've been hit by something infinitely harder than a brick,' Cardish responded absently. 'Thousands of volts of electricity. That does something to a man, remember.'

'Nothing very beneficial from the looks of things!' His wife gave a sniff. 'You're just as moony as you ever were — only more so. If you expect to gain sympathy by keeping up that attitude you're due for a shock! And I don't mean an electric one, either.'

Cardish did not answer. For that matter he did not appear to have heard his wife's remarks. He was gazing through the window on to the flying countryside and trying to reconcile an imponderable riddle in his mind. How was it possible for one man to be in two places at the same time? For that was just what was wrong. By closing his eyes he could vividly see a superb laboratory populated by massive beings with bald heads, olive green skins and pink-tinted eyes. He could also hear everything they were saying, a confusing rippling across his conscious mind. And strangely enough he fancied he was answering them, not so much audibly as mentally. Yes, it was a definite puzzle. Perhaps a hangover from the lightning flash. Perhaps . . .

'I may as well tell you one thing,' Bertha resumed, in her heartless, strident voice, 'and that is that you're changed. Physically, I mean. Nothing much, but the surgeon told me about it in confidence. Can't think why since you're bound to notice it for yourself. Your skin's gone thin since you were struck by lightning. Take a look at your hands.'

'Eh?' Cardish looked at her absently. 'My hands? What's wrong with them?'

'They're thin,' Tommy said deliberately. 'Thin — like your hair is on top. Sort of see through them. Plain horrible, I call it.'

Cardish studied his hands absently. Yes, there was something queer. The veins on the back looked like blue blind cord, twining back into the main arteries. The muscles were almost visible too. With a sudden thought he held his hand to the sunlight and it was as though the flesh were made of tissue paper, so complete was the illusion of transparency.

'Blimey!' Tommy whispered, fascinated. 'Mum, what's gone wrong with him? He's like one of those glass models you see in an outfitters.'

Cardish winced as he lowered his hand. The mention of the word 'outfitters' had reminded him of his daily drudgery, shortly to be resumed.

'I just don't understand it!' Bertha declared. 'Hanged if I do! Why should a flash of lightning make your skin like tracing paper? Isn't even sense!'

'Lightning does strange things,' Cardish told her. 'It has been known to rip your shoes off and leave the rest of you intact. Sometimes it reduces an umbrella to threads, and leaves just the ribs. I even read of a case where it left a man without his trousers.'

Tommy grinned widely, but his mother did not. She tightened her broad nostrils and set about an impatient perusal of the morning paper. So Cardish closed his eyes again and let himself wander.

'There seems little doubt of the fact that some equational freak brought you here, Earthman,' the First in Mathematics commented, as he loomed gigantic amidst the instruments of the major Mazorian laboratory. 'It will be interesting to determine what brought that about — Am I to understand that you are a typical specimen of the male Earth race?'

'Well — er — more or less,' Cardish admitted, with only a slight tremor in his voice. He was recovering from the shattering realization that he was apparently on another planet called Mazor, conversing with its alien inhabitants.

'I see. In that case the race cannot be classed as giants, either physically or mentally. Tell me, are there other roots to your family?'

'Roots?'

'I mean are there parents living? Brothers, sisters, wife, or any such?'

'I have a wife,' Cardish replied slowly. 'And a son. There is also myself.'

'Obviously. You stand there before me.'

'Yes, but I didn't quite mean — That is, I — '

Cardish stopped, chiefly because he was at a loss for words. How the devil was he to explain that all of him was not here on this world? That there was part of him on Earth? Two people, identical, yet ruled by one mind. A kind of Siamese brain.

'You are not very lucid, Earthman,' the Mazorian observed sternly.

'No, I suppose I'm not. Matter of fact I don't know what I'm doing most of the time. I feel sort of dreamlike if you know what I mean.'

'I think I do. The First in Biology has explained that as being a natural reaction to your astonishing experience — ' The Mazorian paused, as though he wondered how best to make himself understood by this very stupid representative of Earth. Then he resumed: 'I think you should know what has happened to you, Earthman. You were caught up in the outflowing energy wave of an inter-dimensional probe, generated from this very laboratory There you behold our master machine.'

Cardish looked — and blinked with incredulity. Occupying a considerable amount of floorage space was the biggest computer he had ever seen. At least it looked like one to his quite unskilled perception. This monstrous instrument, the product of flawless Mazorian genius, was completely lost on the bewildered gent's outfitter from Earth. All he beheld was a titanic array of tubes, screens, insulators and electro-magnets, coupled with miles of heavily insulated wiring. Upon innumerable panels were white recording dials, all of their needles pressed against the zero stops.

'It looks wonderful,' Cardish said, with a weak smile of admiration.

'It is more than that, Earthman, it is the ultimate in mechanical conception. With it we shall understand all dimensions, as we already so well understand time and space in our own world.'

'You mean you can travel in time?' Cardish caught at this possibility quickly. He still remembered how Wells's *Time Machine* had intrigued him as a youth.

'One cannot travel in a mathematical abstraction,' the Mazorian answered coldly. 'And that is all that time really is. We can, however, see what you would regard as future time on Earth with our equipment. Later I may show you — For the moment I feel you should know how you were brought here.'

Cardish was just on the verge of saying that he had not been brought here and that the whole thing was a dream but he checked himself. This couldn't be a dream. It was all too vivid.

'This machine,' the Mazorian explained, 'deals entirely with mathematical vibrations, but in your present stage of intelligence you would not understand that even if I detailed it. We experimented with the machine and it got out of control, generating a powerful wave of mathematical vibrations across dimensions and into your world. During that process parts of your Moon were transposed, which your astronomers will probably notice later — and before that the vibration struck your planet in the region you call the Lake District. To you it seemed like a storm. Actually it was the transfiguration of elemental forces. You were caught up with them and transported here. You came along the vibratory beam itself and reassembled into your present form, re-attuned to our own dimension. Exactly how this happened we don't yet know, but we shall in time. I shall work on the problems myself, and I shall also in time make the dimensional portal completely controllable henceforth.'

'Be just as well,' Cardish agreed, still not having the least conception how he had got here, or even where he was. All the scientific exposition had sailed way over his head.

'In the meantime I can only offer you our sincere apologies for what has happened and give you the free run of our world as compensation.'

'You mean — you mean you can't send me back home? I thought you said that your machine had brought me here? And that you had space travel?'

'Oh, yes, we understand space travel,' the Mazorian agreed dryly. 'But this world exists in a *different dimension* to your Earth, and travel across dimensions involves complications far beyond your comprehension. So far we have only been able to send robotic cameras and monitoring equipment to orbit your planet far out in space — enabling us to study Earth people at fairly close quarters but never as closely as we have studied you. You still insist that you are a good representative of your race?'

'Yes.' Cardish was commencing to feel vaguely proud of himself. 'I would say, though, that no others — or very few — have skin so transparent as mine. Matter of fact it wasn't like this until I — er — left Earth.'

'Probably caused by the mathematical transition you made. No matter. Regarding your question as to whether we can return you to Earth — we can, but we shall not. You have already seen a great deal of our world and we do not wish any of it to be known to an alien race.'

Cardish sighed. 'Can't quite see the point there, sir. I haven't the brains to grasp a tenth of what I've seen. There couldn't be any danger in sending me back home.'

'At this stage we would prefer not to do so.' The Mazorian's powerful face was entirely adamant, the high ceiling lights reflecting from his hairless dome. 'Besides, we wish to observe you closely, see exactly how an Earthman reacts to our different conditions here.'

'I see.' Cardish shrugged. 'Well, maybe it doesn't matter. I'm on Earth whilst I'm here, so it doesn't signify.'

'On Earth whilst here?' The Mazorian looked puzzled. 'I do not understand.'

'Neither do I really. Maybe we'd best forget it — You did say I could have the run of things and look around me?'

'Certainly, and at any time I'll be glad to explain whatever may puzzle you.'

'Which,' Cardish commented, 'will be a full-time job for you, I'm afraid!'

'What will?' Bertha asked harshly. 'For heavens' sake stop talking to yourself! And get the tickets ready, can't you? The inspector's on his way down the corridor.'

Cardish scrambled through the maze of his thoughts to realise he was not only in the Mazorian laboratory but also in a London-bound express. He handed over the tickets as the inspector reached his seat, and through him he could see a high-domed Mazorian and even hear the creature's voice.

'Do you *have* to look so glassy?' Bertha demanded, glaring. 'I don't want the inspector to think I'm travelling with a lunatic, or a sleepwalker.'

'Never tire, do you?' Cardish asked, reflecting. 'Nag, nag, nag, for evermore.'

'Mum's gotta keep you up to scratch, dad!' Tommy declared stoutly, and earned a wide-mouthed smile as his mother glanced at him.

'All I ask,' Cardish said, spreading his hands, 'is the chance to sort myself out after all I've been through. You just don't know what's going on inside me after being in that awful equational disturbance.'

Bertha stared blankly. 'That awful *what*?'

'Storm. Sorry, my mind wandered to something else.'

'I should think it did, coming out with words like that! And as for not knowing what's going on inside you we very soon will if your skin gets any thinner! I still say it's horrible.'

Cardish did not say any more. He merely cherished the hope that perhaps an accident might happen to the train which would leave him a widower and without his son — but the train arrived nearly on time and Bertha and Tommy were as untiring as ever.

Home at least restored some balance to Cardish's mind even though it did not blot out the peculiarly vivid vision of that other world and the Mazorians in the background. It was as though he were constantly looking at a superimposed photograph.

With the passage of the hours the effect did not diminish, either. It had been with him ever since recovering his senses in the hospital, and it began to look as though it might become a permanency. It was frightening and fascinating at the same time. Not being a scientist Cardish did not quite know what to do. His mind revolved round the idea of visiting a psychiatrist. Well later, perhaps, if the effect did not wear off.

Definitely the effect did *not* wear off. Everywhere he went he literally lived two lives, and remarkably enough, conducted both lives simultaneously with a reasonable amount of rationality. On the world of Mazor the experts in science were not in the least aware that the Walter Cardish they had under observation also existed on Earth in absolute duplicate. And on Earth Cardish did not dare mention that he was in two places at once in case somebody called and quietly took him away to a padded cell.

So he settled for a kind of dreamy in-between state, ruling his Mazorian self by what were apparently thought-waves, which in every way activated his Mazorian double, whilst on Earth he tried to behave as he had always done, carefully avoiding any direct explanation for his queer semi-translucent flesh.

Unfortunately, behind the counter of a gentleman's outfitters is not the place to practise a dual personality. The department manager, who had never had much time for Cardish anyhow, could not help noticing the vague way he did things, and the number of mistakes he made. Accordingly he reported the matter to the stores managing director when this overfed individual made his normal weekly visit to compliment or trounce the staff as the case might warrant.

So Cardish came before the bulldog, and looked through him to the wilderness of the Mazorian laboratories beyond.

'I am given to understand, Cardish, that you have not been giving particularly good results lately,' the M.D. said, the swivel chair creaking under his bulk.

'I haven't quite recovered from my accident yet, sir.'

'Accident? Oh, you mean when you were struck by lightning up in the Lake District. Mmmm, unfortunate business, of course, but I remain convinced that by this time you are as physically and mentally fit as you ever will be.'

Cardish did not say anything, which seemed to irritate the M.D. more than somewhat. He harrumphed so violently the ash sprayed from his cigar and lodged in the folds of his waistcoat.

'We can't have it, Cardish,' he said,

with a frank stare. 'Sorry, but that's how it is. I dislike having to tell any of my employees that their work is unsatisfactory, but in your case I am left no alternative.'

'I'm sorry, sir. I hadn't quite realised that I was as — as bad as all that.'

'No, that's where the trouble is, I expect. Always difficult to see ourselves as others see us, eh?' And the M.D. laughed gustily.

'Bit of a relief, sir, sometimes,'

The M.D.'s expression changed abruptly and became malignant.

'Perhaps that was not meant to be impudent, Cardish, but whether it was or not I didn't like it. And also I see no point in delaying matters as far as you are concerned. You are no longer in this company's employ. Collect your salary from the cashier and I'll see to it that you are paid in lieu of notice. I must find somebody more enterprising to take your place.'

'Yes, sir.'

Cardish did not make any fuss or raise any argument. With a dreamy look he turned and left the office. The M.D. watched the door close, frowned to himself, and then picked up the inter-phone to contact the cashier.

2

As he left the great emporium with his final wages, Walter Cardish also strolled leisurely down the great polished halls of the Mazorian laboratories, looking in on large rooms loaded with gigantic machinery. Sometimes he had one of the giant Mazorians beside him as a willing and explanatory mentor; at other times, as now, he walked alone. None of the Mazorians made any attempt to stop him. He passed alien men and women constantly as they went back and forth on various errands.

They either smiled at him courteously or gave directions if he asked for them. Orders had gone forth from the master-scientists that he was in no way to be hindered — that he could examine or operate whatever machinery he wished provided his action did not tend to be dangerous to himself or the Mazorian race.

Altogether, Walter Cardish was well satisfied. He was living in two places at once, certainly; his Mazorian self was constantly under the direction of his Earthly twin, but little by little he was learning how to balance one personality with the other. Which made him unique amongst human beings. He was both present and far away at the same time, and though he was not a wonderfully brilliant man, he could see certain possible advantages to be derived from the situation.

There was for instance this business of viewing future time. He had discovered from his question and answer sessions with the First in Mathematics, that time on Mazor — for reasons that he could not understand — was running approximately 24 hours 'ahead' of Earth time, and he had discovered where they kept the tele-scopic television equipment with which they could see what was happening on Earth.

Apparently the Mazorians — at present, anyway — could only view the Earth from space, where they had spy satellites in orbit. The satellites were hidden from Earth astronomers by some kind of cloaking device. Their cameras could be directed at Earth, and the scenes they saw, because of the different time ratios between the two worlds, were some 24 hours ahead of what the original Walter Cardish was experiencing.

With the close-up lenses in position Earth was so clear that even human beings could be distinguished fairly well. So, with those human beings visible in a *future* time to his Earth self, there might be endless possibilities.

Walter Cardish was determined to explore these possibilities to the uttermost, for what he saw and learned was automatically the property of Walter Cardish of Earth. A fascinating paradox, for which as yet Cardish had no official scientific explanation. To better aid his concentrations, Cardish did not return home immediately. He would only meet the bleak enquiries of Bertha if he did: so instead he turned into the public library and took advantage of the reading room's silence to explore mentally the scientific wilderness in that other world.

He found he could not hope to understand the Mazorian satellite viewing equipment without assistance, but this was readily forthcoming from the saturnine First in Mathematics. He seemed to take a delight in airing his profound knowledge and confounding the few wits of the miserable Earthman.

Cardish well knew this, but he never showed resentment

He knew something that high-and-mighty First of Mathematics did *not* know; namely, that he was two people at once and learning all about Mazor and the Mazorians in the most unique way ever. Just what the high-domed First in Mathematics would have done had he guessed the truth Cardish did not dare to think.

'If I am to remain here for the rest of my life,' Cardish said, deliberately adopting a wheedling tone, 'I would love to be able to view my home country of England, and to follow the social and other pursuits of my fellows. It would help me to overcome my loneliness. Is your wonderful science capable of enabling me to view places in England or the rest of the world that can give me comfort and pleasure? Or would such a miracle be beyond even you?'

His last remark was carefully calculated to appeal to the First's colossal ego — and it did.

'What is an apparent miracle to you, Earthman, is an everyday achievement for my race,' the first commented loftily. 'Would I be right in assuming that once you had identified these areas of your country you wanted to view, you would wish to view them again in subsequent days?'

'Oh yes — again and again!' Cardish said, thinking ahead to the scheme he was evolving.

'Then I will accommodate you. It will be a relatively simple matter. It will involve moving one of our many spy satellites into a geo-synchronous orbit over England.' He smiled cynically at Cardish's expression.

'To view the same part of the Earth below, the satellite simply needs to match its orbital speed with the rotation of the

Earth. Because you are so mechanically inept, the settings on the viewing mechanism will have to be automatic. I will seek the help of the First in Electronics to incorporate into the equipment a self-thinking device, and a small panel with simple selection controls with symbols in your own language. You can use you own control panel to both roam across the planet — picking up overlapping images from our several satellites as they cover all of the planet — whilst your own country of England will always be constantly in view should you require it. Once you have fixed on a location it will be stored in the machine's memory, so that you can return to view it again at any time.'

'Thank you,' Cardish said, and meant it.

'When we wish to view any area on Earth we switch on the power and to the spot under examination we direct a beam of energy. This beam works much as your childish radar does, reflecting back into the mechanism an 'echo' of the scene it has struck. This 'echo' image is dealt with by the dimensional-determinators within each satellite, which change its vibration level to our own, and finally there appears on this screen here a picture of the exact spot, transmitted from your dimension to ours.'

Cardish looked at the presently blank viewing screen and groped around the profound intricacies. Finally he gave a rather troubled smile.

'Naturally, sir, I don't understand one half of what you're talking about, but I gather from what you told me earlier that what I'd see on the screen is 24 hours ahead of what I would have seen if I had remained on Earth and never came here?'

'Yes. It is because of our different time ratios. When we send our satellites into orbit and move them into your dimension, they 'emerge' some 24 hours ahead of the time-line you were originally living in.'

'That's marvellous!' Cardish whispered. 'The most wonderful scientific thing I ever heard of. But I don't quite see why your viewing of the Earth has to be from a satellite. Why can't you also view things down here at ground level? Or am I asking too many questions?'

'Ask whatever you wish. It is only natural that one so low in intellect must have many interrogations to put forward. The answer to your question has to do with the scientific fact that co-relative states of matter — such as Mazor and Earth — can only exist within the confines of a material world,' the Mazorian scientist explained. 'Matter-within-matter exists only where there is a planet. And between those worlds there exists a normally impenetrable barrier of differing rates of vibration. But that barrier decreases when one travels into space, where matter as such virtually ceases to exist in any appreciable quantity. There, the barrier is relatively thin. With a relatively small expenditure of energy, people on objects from different vibratory planes can — by increasing or decreasing their vibratory rate — cross over and meet on a common level, because space isn't part of their inherent vibratory set-ups. You follow, Earthman?'

'I think so.' Cardish was concentrating intently. His scheme depended on his understanding enough to make it workable.

'To carry out the same transition at or near ground level requires vastly more potentially destructive energy, difficult to control. Our recent experiment to try and achieve this was not entirely successful.'

'As I know only too well!' Cardish commented dryly. 'Vast electrical storms were created in the Lake District in my world. I was caught up in the midst of it, and ended up here!'

'From which accident we have extracted much valuable data,' the First in Mathematics remarked enigmatically. 'And when we have fully analysed it, we shall — ' He suddenly broke off, and tightened his lips.

'Shall what?'

'That is none of your business, and quite beyond your comprehension.' The Mazorian appeared angry that he should have been on the verge of imparting information he clearly did not want Cardish to know. 'Do you want me to construct your Earth-viewing apparatus?' he snapped.

Cardish realized it would be unwise for him to continue with his question.

'Yes, of course. I would be very grateful. To occupy and to amuse myself I've a feeling I'd like to see my world as it might look 24 hours hence.'

'You can try it by all means. As long as you are here with us in our world you cannot do any harm.'

In the library back on Earth Walter Cardish gave a little start and looked about him. Somebody with a noisy cough had disturbed his concentrations, but it had not destroyed his dual identity. Nothing could apparently.

'Psychiatrist?' he muttered. 'I wonder now — '

Finally he made up his mind. Fifteen minutes later he was within the ornate chamber of Dr. Howard Dantill, describing himself on the brass plate as 'Psychiatrist, Psychologist and Expert on Juvenile Delinquency'. Cardish wondered about two things as he sat in the waiting room. Should he be here, or his son Tommy?

Then the blonde in the revealing white

overall returned and smiled dazzlingly.

'Dr. Dantill will see you now, Mr. Cardish. Will you step this way, please?'

Cardish rose and entered a sunny office, sparsely furnished with only one light oak desk and a very long chesterfield. At the desk sat a broad-shouldered man with upswept black hair and piercing light-blue eyes.

'Ah, Mr. Cardish! How *are* you!'

'Not so good I'm afraid, otherwise I wouldn't be here.'

The psychiatrist rose, came round the desk, and then pumped Cardish's hand fiercely.

'You'll forgive me, Mr. Cardish, if I don't ask you to sit down? I'm a man of action and most of my work is done on a chesterfield. Be good enough to lie on it.'

Meekly Cardish did as ordered, lying full length and relaxing, his head supported on a silk cushion. Howard Dantill loomed over him, immaculate, reeking of lavender water, his eyes like black currants set in pearl buttons. Cardish did not know whether he was a phony or genuine: he had simply picked him out of the telephone directory. In any case he considered all psychiatrists as damned interlopers upon one's privacy.

'Now, sir!' Dantill clasped his hands behind him, 'What seems to be the trouble?'

'The trouble is that I'm in two places at once. I'm two people and yet I'm one. More clearly, I'm one mind ruling two bodies and it gets very confusing.'

'Hmmm.' Or something like it.

'I've been like this ever since being struck by lightning. You remember that Lakeland storm recently? I was in it — in the very centre. According to the doctors I got something like ninety thousand volts through me. Miracle is that I'm alive.'

'Hmmm.'

'Over to you now,' Cardish said wearily. 'Ask me anything you like. Better still try and solve what's wrong.'

'That may take time. I shall have to delve into your inhibitions, secret vices, buried urges and debased promptings. Are you married, Mr. Cardish?'

'I am. I have a son nearing manhood. I'll be frank, doctor. I'd like to see my

41

wife and son at the bottom of the sea.'

'Your frankness does you credit, sir.' Dantill made a note. 'We have there the probable motivating cause of your mental aberration. Hatred can definitely induce strange quirks of the mind.'

'Maybe, but I still think a flash of lightning through me is the main trouble.'

'I see. Tell me, where exactly is this other self you refer to? Or rather where do you imagine it is?'

'It's not a case of imagination — it actually exists. On another planet called Mazor.'

The psychiatrist opened his mouth and then stared. 'Did you say '*Mazor*'? I never heard of such a planet!'

'Nor me. But that's their name for it. I know for a fact that I am the guest, or rather the captive of the ruling scientists of Mazor. They are polite and treat me with every courtesy, telling me all I want to know because they believe my Mazorian self is the only one in existence. If they knew I was here as well they'd be more careful. I've already learnt a lot.'

'Most extraordinary! Such as?'

'That Lakeland storm for one thing. It wasn't really a storm — it was an outburst of badly controlled mathematics as far as I can gather.'

Dr. Howard Dantill was now definitely up against it — and his expression showed it, but not for long. He was experienced enough to cover up his confusion by scribbling industriously in his notebook.

'Mazor — storm — outburst of mathematics,' he repeated solemnly. 'Definitely a most extraordinary case.'

'I don't expect you to believe me,' Cardish apologised. 'No normal man would. But I can't go on hugging this amazing problem to myself. I've got to have advice. How do I cut free from my other self?'

'I cannot advise you regarding that, sir, until I am sure that you have one — and you say this *alter ego* is on another world. I have very little chance of substantiating your claim.'

'Can't you take my word for it that it is so?'

'I can — and I do. But it is not enough. As a psychiatrist, I must have the incontestable evidence laid before me. To be quite candid, Mr. Cardish, I never heard of a case like yours in all my experience. I would say it is impossible for two bodies to be controlled by one mind, or will.'

'Why impossible? A hypnotist controls a subject and his own body as well at one and the same time. It ought even to be *easier* for a person to control himself and his double simultaneously.'

The piercing eyes became masked with thought. 'True, sir — true. A clever pointer — However, I would not be honest if I said I could help you, because I cannot. Yours is not a case of straightforward split personality, or even twin duality. It is absolutely unprecedented — Do you mean you are this other person during your sleeping hours?'

'Good heavens, no! I'm the other Walter Cardish all the time! At this very moment I can see around you the wonderful laboratories of Mazor and even the Mazorians themselves as they move about their tasks. Nothing has a definite solidity any more. I found it confusing at first but now I'm getting more used to it.'

The psychiatrist ran an immaculate finger along his lower lip and took professional refuge in profound meditation. It was more convincing than his admitting he didn't know what the hell to say next.

'Look at my hands,' Cardish resumed. 'All of me is just the same. Glass-like. You can nearly see the bone and muscle structure. My wife says it's horrible.'

'I would be inclined to say unique.' The psychiatrist stooped and examined Cardish's hand intently; then a gleam came into his pale eyes. 'I have said, Mr. Cardish, that I find your case outside my scope because of lack of proof on which to build my diagnosis. But I know a man who might be able to help you. He's a physical scientist, and in all truth I think that is the kind of person you need. It is not just your mentality which seems disturbed — your body as well is transformed.'

Cardish straightened up from the chesterfield. 'Where do I find him?'

'You have no need to. I'll have him over

here in a few minutes.'

Dantill turned to the telephone and whipped it up. He spoke to somebody by the name of Gascoyne, referred to an amazing case, and finally secured the promise of the said Gascoyne to come over immediately. Thereafter Dantill did not even refer to the case. Plainly he had thrown it overboard as too complex for him to deal with.

Pleasantries were exchanged, and then at length the dazzling blonde reappeared to usher in a short man with a spiky moustache and cream-and-roses complexion.

'Mr. Cardish — Dr. Gascoyne,' Dantill introduced, and the little scientist shook hands vigorously.

'Glad to know you, Mr. Cardish. The man who was struck by lightning in that Lakeland storm, I believe?'

'Er — yes.' Cardish looked surprised. 'I don't recall Dr. Dantill mentioning the fact on the phone.'

'He didn't. I happen to be one of the scientists engaged on research concerning that storm, therefore I know all the names of the people mixed up in it. You, I believe, were more affected than anybody?'

'I was — ' And Cardish told his story all over again, in more detail this time. By the time he had finished Gascoyne was seated at the other end of the chesterfield, his plump little hands pressed palm down on his fat thighs as he meditated.

'Unusual,' he said. 'But not impossible. Certainly you won't get the answer from Dantill here. This business goes right into physical science.'

'Just what I said!' Dantill looked relieved. 'I realised that from the moment I saw our friend's skin. It's as transparent as parchment.'

'So I've noticed. That could be caused by electronic change.'

Cardish looked as though he had really heard something worthwhile at last.

'Can you amplify that, Dr. Gascoyne?'

'With pleasure, but before I get to that, we need to consider how this world of Mazor — this parallel Earth — can exist alongside our own, invisible and undetected — except by you! It is because of the nature of our atomic universe!

'The atom,' Gascoyne went on, 'is best described by the schoolboy who declared it was a pattern held together by holes. More scientifically, it means that there is nothing in matter that is really solid. Any matter object, when you analyse it down, is mainly empty space. The material part we see is basically composed of electric charges analogous to miniature solar systems, with electrons circling a protonic nucleus. And, in the electronic space, the distances are quite comparable with those between our world and the nearest star. So then, matter is mainly holes. Right?'

'I follow — I think.' Cardish shrugged. 'Where does it get us?'

'It gets us to the solution to your problem. If another form of matter — or indeed *many* forms of matter — fitted into the space which is empty we'd have other worlds and other people existing parallel to ourselves, but invisible to us.'

Cardish frowned, remembering something he had once read as a boy. 'But surely no two bodies can occupy the same space at the same time?'

'Quite right,' Gascoyne smiled. 'If they tried to, there'd be a tremendous explosion. But Earth and Mazor are *not* co-existing in the same space. They're in a *different* space, living at a different vibratory rate.'

'You mean that space may really be a kind of jigsaw?' Dantill questioned, frowning.

'Precisely! Imagine your jigsaw without several of the main pieces, and there you have a typical example of a chunk of matter — mainly holes. Fit the corresponding patterns of the jigsaw into the missing spaces and the thing is complete. Space is really not empty at all. Other existences, people, and worlds march invisibly alongside one another.'

'All very interesting,' Cardish sighed, 'but it doesn't explain how part of me got into this other world of Mazor — '

'I'm coming to that!' Gascoyne said. 'I believe that under tremendous electrical stimulus a given material object may be compelled to part with half its quota of molecules.'

Cardish's brow wrinkled. 'I'm a gent's

outfitter by trade. You're talking way above me, Dr. Gascoyne.'

'I apologise. Try it this way: every material object is made up of a given number of atoms, which when grouped are called molecules. You understand that?'

'Yes, that's plain enough.'

'Very well then. Your body, my body, every material object, is made up like that. Molecules are basically electrical and therefore subject to electrical reaction. It has been shown over and over again in the physical laboratories that under tremendously high voltage molecules tear apart. It has not been shown that they divide into exact halves, for that would be too much to detect with our present instruments, but it is believed by many scientists that this indeed may happen. I am inclined to think that in your case an astounding combination of circumstances brought this very phenomenon about.'

'You — you mean I split in two?' Cardish looked dazed, at which the plump little scientist smiled.

'Not exactly in the sense that you mean it. More correctly, each molecule in your body divided itself and therefore was bound to form into an identical counterpart of yourself but with a loss of density. Since only half of your molecular basis remains you appear almost transparent — and so possibly does your double.'

'He does. I know that much.'

'There it is then. A combination of intense electrical voltage, together with this Mazorian business of mathematical transpositions, produced an amazing phenomenon and divided you into two halves instead of killing you outright. One half was withdrawn to the Mazorian source along this mathematical beam, or whatever it was, and the other half remained. Your mind controls both bodies because actually you are only controlling the same amount of matter as before, the difference being that it is in two different places.'

'I'll be damned!' Dantill said frankly, perched on the edge of the desk. 'And what does our friend do to get himself right again?'

Gascoyne shook his head. 'That's something I can't answer. You must remember that this business is utterly unprecedented so I can't be expected to predict how it will work out. In one way you are to be congratulated, Mr. Cardish, for proving a scientific theory to be correct. In another you are to be pitied for your unfortunate predicament.'

Cardish nodded gloomily. 'I'm wondering, Dr. Gascoyne, why you accept my story so completely. Dr. Dantill had his doubts, and I don't blame him.'

'I accept your story because I know it is true, and I'll tell you why. You mentioned in relating your experiences that the Mazorians have said that their mathematical beam transposed certain portions of the moon's surface. That, my dear sir, is a fact. I know that from my own investigations. Tycho has changed places with Copernicus, to be exact, and every astronomer in the world has been racking his brains to understand why. Now, that fact has not been published. You could not possibly have known of it, and yet you gave the information. That is why I know you speak truth.'

'I assume,' Dantill put in, 'that you won't go any further, Gascoyne, in trying to solve the mystery of the Lakeland storm?'

'Be a waste of time,' the scientist agreed, rising. 'We have the full answer from our friend here, and the sooner the world knows how extraordinary a man he is, the better.'

'I would much prefer,' Cardish said slowly, 'that you did not publish anything at all.'

'But my dear sir!' Dantill protested. 'You can be famous. Worth a fortune, probably, for the information you can sell.'

'Yes, yes, I know, but consider my position, gentlemen. I am also on Mazor at this very moment. The Mazorians believe the man they see is the only one in existence — a quite natural assumption. For that reason they have been extremely free with their information, and by degrees, I am learning many secrets of science, which will later benefit our race. Also don't forget that they can hear our radio broadcasts quite easily. If they find

Walter Cardish of Earth is getting a lot of limelight because he is two people my number will probably be up. I don't quite know what would happen if my double got killed and not I myself, but possibly the mental shock would finish me anyhow. On top of that the Mazorians might consider they had been hoaxed and they'd descend on Earth in all their fury — Against them we wouldn't stand a chance. No, there must not be any publicity.'

'He's right,' Dantill said, as he and Gascoyne exchanged grave looks.

'Yes, I'm afraid so,' Gascoyne made the admission grudgingly. 'Very well, Mr. Cardish, we'll keep it dark as far as the public is concerned, but every scientist in the land must know the facts — confidentially, of course. You need have no fear. Scientists are an honest body of men, and nothing will leak out. I see clearly how it would jeopardise not only you but the whole human race if the Mazorians found out the truth. As a matter of interest, what do you yourself propose to do about the situation?'

Cardish smiled enigmatically. 'At the moment I'm not quite sure — but I do know I shall continue learning Mazorian secrets as long as I'm permitted, and I'll pass them on to you, Dr. Gascoyne, for our scientists to handle. As for the personal side I have a very strong desire to one day show these cocksure Mazorians that I'm not quite the ignorant fool they take me for. You have no conception how it rankles with me to be constantly treated like a child of seven by a very superior headmaster — Yes,' Cardish finished slowly, 'I'll make them sit up one day. I can, you know, because I have the master-key. They're just giving away their knowledge all over the place.'

'We'll look forward to anything you can tell us,' Gascoyne said promptly. 'Where you find the Mazorian science too deep for you just memorise as much of the details as you can and we'll have our own expert scientists ferret out the rest.'

'Done!' Cardish held out his hand. 'I feel a great deal better now, gentlemen, thanks to your advice and suggestions.

You'll hear more of me — Oh, what do I owe you?'

'Far as I am concerned, nothing.' Dantill said. 'I did not do anything beyond calling in Gascoyne.'

'And as far as I am concerned I consider myself repaid by meeting you,' the scientist smiled. 'Whenever you wish to contact me I can be reached at the Society for Physical Research in Kensington.'

Cardish nodded and upon that took his departure, smiling a farewell — not without reluctance — to the blonde-haired receptionist behind her little desk in the outer office.

Certainly it was no blonde-haired receptionist who greeted Cardish upon his arrival home at about the usual time. It was Bertha — massive and grim-faced as usual as she palavered about with some enigmatic form of cooking in the kitchenette.

'You're before time,' she stated bluntly, as Cardish poked his head into the blue fumes. 'That being so, don't start grumbling if your tea isn't on the table.

56

I'm not a magician.'

'True,' Cardish admitted, sighing — and withdrew.

When Bertha had finally got the chops fried beyond recognition she came into the living room with them to find Cardish seated beside the window, staring out on to the weed-choked garden. The clatter of crockery startled him.

'What are you mooning about?' Bertha asked briefly. 'Be more to the point if you got the garden to rights, wouldn't it?'

'Anything wrong with Tommy doing it?'

'Everything! He's only young yet and he might give himself a nasty internal wrench with that stupid mower. Then where would he be?'

Cardish could think of many possible places but he refrained from mentioning them. He turned wearily from the window and sat at the table, saying nothing as the incinerated chop was laid before him.

'Can't help it,' Bertha said irritably, as though she had guessed his reaction. 'The stove's too fierce. Been like that ever since those gas company fools repaired the griller — Truth is, we need a new stove, but I suppose I might as well ask for the moon.'

Cardish prodded the chop experimentally with his fork

'If you're wondering where Tommy is — '

'I'm not. I couldn't care less.'

'Nice thing to say about your own son! Honestly, Walter, the more I live with you the less I know of you.'

'That,' Cardish said, 'is probably true. And you'll find you'll know less and less as time goes on. Things have happened to me since that storm in the Lake District.'

'You don't have to tell me that!' Bertha poured out the tea tilting the pot viciously in her effort to hurry the procedure. 'And Tommy's playing cricket on Tanner's Field. I told him to go there because you start whining when he smashes the neighbour's windows with cricket balls.'

Cardish chewed remorselessly at the tough end of his chop.

'I got fired today,' he said presently.

'Oh!' Bertha started violently. 'You *what?*'

'I said I got fired. The department manager sneaked up on me and reported that I wasn't doing my job properly. Result — dismissal.'

'And you sit there and calmly admit it? What are you going to do about it? How are we going to live? Your bank balance won't keep us going for long.'

Cardish smiled mysteriously to himself, quite glad of the fact that he had given Bertha a real blow to the heart at last. There was something gratifying in seeing her looking scared for once.

'Well, well?' she demanded. 'What are we going to do? You'll have to look for a fresh job right away. The evening paper will be here anytime and then you can — '

'Not likely!' Cardish still chewed the same piece of chop with untiring determination.

'What do you mean? — not likely! You *must*!'

'The man who works for other people is a fool, Bertha. Any successful man will tell you that. The thing to do is to cash in on your gifts and be your own master.'

'But you haven't any gifts! I never knew a man so dull or un-enterprising. That's what makes me so mad at you.'

'Oh?' Cardish looked surprised. 'So that's the reason? Well, I'll let you into a secret, Bertha. The job I had at the store doesn't mean a thing any more. I'd have left anyway because I've discovered that since being struck by lightning I can foretell the future.'

'Eh?'

'I can see what is going to happen. I can see ahead.'

Bertha did not say anything. She really believed with all her heart that her husband's strange manner since the storm had at last crystallised into visible insanity. Yes, he was going off it. No other answer.

'I can see 24 hours ahead of now,' Cardish continued, at last masticating the piece of chop. 'No great event can happen without my knowing in advance. As to how I do it — well. That's my secret. My gift.'

'You're barmy!' Bertha decided, with refreshing candour.

'I expected that from you, Bertha. You can't see beyond the end of your nose. You're one of the dimwits who need proof hammered in with a chisel before you'll believe. You'll get that proof, believe me!'

'Huh!' Bertha said, and as if this was not expressive enough she added a further '*Huh!*' after a moment or two.

Cardish remained undisturbed, He continued with the burnt offering, chewing until his jaws ached and finally washing the lot down with tea. This done he got up from the table and went again to the window, staring out on to the garden.

Bertha watched him, her unhealthy-looking face shining with the warmth of the day and the reaction of the meal.

'What on earth do you keep looking out of the window for?' she asked crossly. 'Get the garden straightened up — don't just look at it!'

'I'm not looking at it. I'm looking at a machine.'

Dead silence.

'A machine far away,' Cardish whispered, exulting. 'It can tell me everything

I want to know. It will always tell me everything I want to know. With it I can see the future — Do you realise how much power that gives me?'

'Don't you think,' Bertha ventured, 'that you'd better see a doctor? You're not talking rationally, Walter.'

'I know it and I'm proud of it! I like to see you scared for once. Just a little repayment for the years of nagging you've given me — '

Bertha did not speak — not because she couldn't but because Tommy came banging in at that moment, flinging down a cricket bat noisily into a corner.

''Lo, dad! Mooning around as usual! Don't you ever do any serious work?'

Cardish turned slowly. Tommy glanced at his mother.

'Where's my tea, ma? I'm hungry!'

'If you want your tea you'll come in at a proper time and get it,' Cardish stated flatly. 'You can wait now until suppertime. Meanwhile, get outside and straighten the garden.'

'Who? Me?' Tommy stared, lips outthrust

'You! *Now!*'

For a second or two the silence was absolute. Tommy could not possibly know that his father was just commencing to realise what vast, terrifying power he had in his hands; he could not know that his father was suddenly alive to the fact that he was different from all other men on Earth and therefore entitled to respect. The day of the worm was over . . .

'All right,' Tommy said at last, sullenly, and mooched out into the garden.

'You had no right — ' Bertha began, but Cardish cut her short.

'Bertha, if I were a gentleman I'd ask you to cease talking so much. Since I don't pretend to be a gentleman I'll let you have it straight — *Shut up!*'

Bertha blinked, her face shinier than ever.

'And stay that way,' Cardish added coldly. 'From here on you're no longer the wife of an outfitter. You're the wife of the greatest seer the world has ever known. God knows whether you'll live up to it, but I'm hoping. In any event you do as I say from here on — or get out and take Tommy with you. Understand?'

'Walter, I'm sure you need a doctor — '

'Don't be ridiculous.' Cardish turned from the window and there came the noise of the mower outside. 'I have been given a gift through being struck by lightning, and I'm going to make it pay the ultimate in dividends. You need proof, of course, so try this: Tomorrow morning as near as I can judge by the night shadow across the Earth, a strato-cruiser numbered A-64 bound from New York to London will crash-land in Heathrow, its engines on fire.'

'Yes?' Bertha's face was sullen, her voice dubious. 'Why don't you warn them if you're so sure?'

'Because I can't alter what Time says will happier. And there might be survivors.'

There were. Everybody was saved. The 6 p.m. radio and TV bulletins next day carried the A-64 disaster for their headlines and Bertha Cardish was quite the most dumbfounded woman in Britain . . .

3

So, in a modest way, Walter Cardish changed his course in life from gentlemen's outfitting to prognostication. Nobody except Bertha knew of his astonishing feat in predicting the A-64 disaster, and this was quite sufficient to convince her at least that her husband was mysteriously gifted. It frightened her so much she too changed her tactics by talking less and helping more. Dominated by these changed beings Tommy could only do exactly as he was told, which made his petulant lips stick out all the more in consequence.

Of course, the prediction business was quite simple. The Mazorian 'time-telescope' (as Cardish mentally dubbed it) was directly responsible and the Mazorian version of Walter Cardish was commencing to enjoy himself no end. He had recovered from the strain of trying to control two entities simultaneously and his system was now complete. Respite came when he slept, because his double slept at the same time. He had achieved a balance, and he worked to a definite end. He meant knowing all about Mazor there was to know, and he also meant to benefit his Earth self not a little.

For a couple of weeks he experimented with trifling predictions as the Mazorian telescope revealed them, but he did not publish his forecasts beyond his home. Every time they inevitably came true and Bertha's wonder increased by leaps and bounds. Tommy was not told anything to commence with in case he talked too much amongst the uncouth sub-human young men whom he had for friends.

At the end of the two weeks Cardish dipped into his modest bank account and rented a city office. Outside it he put a brass plate:

THE GREAT VOLTA
PROGNOSTICATOR EXTRAORDINARY

Apart from the grey hairs developed by the sign writer in spelling such jaw-crackers, everything was in order. All that was required now was a bit of publicity, and for this Cardish turned to his friend Dr. Gascoyne.

Gascoyne's response was to visit the office in person, where Cardish proudly showed him around. There was both a reception office and the private one, this latter furnished in a semi-oriental style and bringing an aroma of the East into grey old London.

'Not bad, eh?' Cardish asked, rubbing his hands.

'Decidedly good. Must have put you back quite a penny.'

'I'll make it up later, dozens of times over. Have a seat, Gascoyne. I feel you're the only man I can talk to safely. My wife and son just don't understand and there's nobody else. You understand?'

'Of course.' Gascoyne seated himself.

'You're probably wondering,' Cardish said, 'why I've called myself the 'Great Volta' instead of using my own name.'

'I can guess. You feel it is safer to have a pseudonym if you become famous later through your prognostications.'

'That's it. The name 'Volta' refers to the number of volts I got through me with that lightning flash. However, the main issue at the moment is publicity. I need plenty of it, and I *don't* want my own name known in case it reaches the media and then the Mazorians. Any suggestions?'

'Well, now — ' Gascoyne thought for a moment. 'It seems to me that you'll have more chance of reaching the heart of the public if you forecast something which is within their sphere of activity, and by which they can perhaps make a personal profit. For instance — horse racing.'

'You think that would be a sounder proposition than waiting for the prediction of a great flood, or an earthquake somewhere?'

'Dammit, man, you might have to wait ages for a freak of Nature like that — and mankind doesn't profit from it anyway. From sure fire racing tips you could make a fortune in no time, both from your own betting and your fees for tips.'

'You don't think that is rather a come-down?'

'It's never a come-down to make money,' Gascoyne said with conviction.

'Don't try and be fancy, Cardish. Do something everybody can understand. That is if it is feasible to forecast horse racing. How about this Mazorian telescopic camera? Is it powerful enough to enable you to pick out individual horses and their numbers from its orbit out in space?'

'Not quite, but I *can* read the results board quite clearly. I have already done so. The telescope is not quite strong enough to identify actual horses or people — '

'I should think not! The miracle to me is how the devil these Mazorians have installed their spy satellites and our astronomers and astronauts have never detected them.'

Cardish shrugged. 'They told me they're fitted with some kind of electronic cloaking device which renders them invisible — even to radar. They're many thousands of years ahead of us in accomplishment, remember. To get back to the point — I forecast horse racing, every time correctly. Anything else?'

'Yes. How about the much easier job of

weather forecasting? We could do with some really infallible forecasts for a change. The meteorologists do their best, I know, but with a crazy climate like we've got even they make mistakes. Manage that?'

'I think so,' Cardish assented, musing. 'If I see clouds over certain parts of Earth I shan't know whether rain is descending from them or not, but possibly the Mazorians will have a way of knowing. I'll see what I can do. Any other angles?'

'How about the stock market?'

Cardish shook his head. 'No use. Most of the stock market deals take place inside buildings, and in any case I wouldn't be able to pinpoint any market results anywhere — not after the style of a race meeting board, for instance. No, that's out. I should imagine I've all I need with weather forecasting and horse racing. Later, when the season starts, I can forecast all the football matches.'

'And for good measure throw in startling occurrences, such as big fires, floods, accidents, and so forth. You'd even gain public sympathy and gratitude if you warned against such and such a train, or plane, being patronised because of accident.'

'Mmmm.' Cardish looked bothered. 'I'm in rather a quandary concerning accidents, Gascoyne, and here's why: if I see them in the future they will happen just as I see them, and if I see people involved in them those people will be involved in that no matter what warning I may give. Time can't be changed. Whatever I see in the future is there.'

'I see your point.' Gascoyne looked disappointed. 'Well, there it is. Better steer clear of accidents, then, at least until we've evolved a foolproof approach — ' He smiled with some apology. 'I say 'we', but perhaps I'm assuming too much? Maybe you won't wish to consider me as a kind of unofficial partner?'

'I'm only too glad to have you at my back!' Cardish declared fervently. 'A thing like this is too big for me to handle by myself — For the time being I'll try and get things going myself. Once I've done so we'll talk again and probably expand. How's that?'

'Excellent!' Gascoyne rose and shook hands. 'Best of luck.'

On the strength of which Cardish went into action with a series of advertisements, and since there are always suckers willing to take a chance he was by no means disappointed with the answers he got. He tackled the horse racing to begin with, making a note through his Mazorian entity of the race meeting boards for one day hence. Thus equipped he was ready to do business — even though, on Mazor itself the inscrutable scientists of that planet wondered vaguely at the Earthworm's profound interest in scampering quadrupeds.

'You really believe,' asked the florid woman, who was one of Cardish's first clients, 'that you can correctly forecast every winner in all the races at Redcar tomorrow?'

Cardish smiled modestly. 'My dear madam, I can forecast them anywhere.'

'But suppose they are scratched before the race, or develop blind staggers, or something like that?'

'The horses I select, madam, always run. The Great Volta is incapable of making a mistake.'

The florid woman could be forgiven for looking as though she doubted it. However, her luck on the gee-gees had been atrocious lately, and there seemed no harm in giving this mild-mannered pundit a trial.

'I'd like the winners of the two-thirty, three-thirty and four o'clock,' she said finally. 'What's your charge?'

'One hundred pounds per race, madam. Or one hundred per horse, which amounts to the same thing.'

'A hundred pounds!' The woman jumped as though she'd been stung. 'Three hundred for three tips! You deserve jail for a swindle like that.'

Cardish only smiled. 'My dear madam, I am not a swindler, I am the only seer who dares to offer a money-back guarantee. If my predictions do not come true you shall have your money back to the last penny.'

'Just — just how can you be so sure?' The florid woman was looking worried. 'It has a sort of uncanny ring about it.'

'Let us say, dear madam, that I am not

as other men. Now, you have my terms, do you wish to do business? I have many more clients waiting.'

The woman hesitated. 'You sound convincing enough, Mr. Volta, but three hundred pounds is an awful lot for me to risk — '

'Madam, I insist there *is* no risk. If it would make you any happier I'm prepared to take a post-dated cheque for my fee, a cheque that I cannot cash until the winners are known. Should I prove wrong, which is impossible, you will have time to stop the cheque before I cash it.'

'That,' said the florid woman, 'is good enough for me!'

Out came her chequebook from a capacious handbag — which seemed to give the lie to the fact that she had not much money — and within a moment or two Cardish found the cheque in his hands. He studied it, nodded, and then consulted his file.

'The horses, madam, are Colt's Foot, Stench of Mystery and Bacon Slicer.'

'They can't be! They're all rank outsiders.'

'Nevertheless, that is the answer. I hope you will come again madam — and thank you for your patronage.'

Thus dismissed the florid woman departed and the next client came in. If ever there was money for jam, Cardish reflected this must be it. Simply by looking through a telescope and adjusting a few controls that had been especially fitted to make the operation simple, he was able to have a rain of cheques descending upon him. And nothing, absolutely nothing, could make him predict incorrectly The only thing that *could* upset his activity was a failure of his eyesight, but after all there was nothing wrong with it at the moment, and if anything did develop the Mazorians were brilliant enough in surgery to perhaps put his Mazorian self right again anyway . . .

Silly conjecture in the midst of plenty!

From his first day's activity Cardish found himself the possessor of £40,600, so fickle is the public when it thinks it is on a sure thing. In this case there was no doubt about it, but not a single man or woman who had parted with a cheque knew that. Which said much for the trusting nature of the majority.

'Forty thousand six hundred pounds!' Bertha repeated dazedly, when she heard of it over the evening meal. 'But — but it isn't right, Walter! You'll be in jail next!'

'Don't be ridiculous! I can't use one of these cheques until tomorrow is over — that safeguards me. On the other hand I shall simply be proven exactly right, and no law in the land can touch a man for that — Pass me the sugar.'

Bertha handed it absently. 'You — you sort of do all this forecasting because lightning hit you on the noodle? Is that it?'

'To accomplish these feats I'm going through a great deal, both physically and mentally. Don't ask me to explain because I don't intend to. Just be grateful I stick by you now — when I could easily cut away.'

'You'll be getting the cops after you, dad, 'fore you're finished, just as mum says!' Tommy declared, his eyes steel bright at the thought. ''Sides, there'll be a lot of turn-ups in the racing tomorrow.

It's going to be bone-dry everywhere and that'll make the going tricky.'

'For a lad of your age you know a good deal about it,' Cardish commented. 'And it won't be bone dry, either.'

'Course it will! The weather forecast said so at six o'clock.'

'It will rain everywhere!' Cardish said flatly, then struck with a thought he rose from the table. 'Be back in a moment; I have just thought of something. And the sooner we get a telephone extension in here the better.'

He left the room and went to the hall telephone. He rang the number of the *Daily Flashlight* and waited.

'City editor,' he requested, when a sing-song voice answered him.

Pause, whirring noises, twang — 'City editor speaking. Be brief and articulate if you please.'

'This is the Great Volta,' Cardish said calmly. 'You may have heard of me.'

'And I may not. Sorry. What can I do for you?'

'I can give you an interesting news item. A little while ago you ran an advertisement of mine — the Great Volta, Prognosticator Extraordinary — that is why I've selected you for a tit-bit.'

'Very grateful. What is it?'

'It will rain everywhere in England tomorrow.'

'Who the hell cares?'

'You misunderstand, sir. The weather forecasters tonight have stated it will remain dry all over England. I, the Great Volta, say unequivocally that they are incorrect. It will be a country-wide deluge. Volta versus the weather forecasters. Is that news or isn't it?'

'Might be worth an inch,' the news editor agreed. 'Okay. I'll gamble.'

'It's worth more than an inch!' Cardish insisted. 'The weather is the most talked-of topic in England. Make a splash with it.'

'Sorry. I'm running this paper, Mr. Volta, not you — and I know just how much room I've got, 'Bye.'

Cardish grimaced as the line became dead. Somewhat gloomily he returned to the kitchen and finished his meal. Bertha and Tommy both waited for him to explain himself but apparently nothing was forthcoming.

Finally Tommy took his departure to some unnamed recreation ground and the young men and women who frequented it. Cardish still sat on, looking through the crockery as Bertha moved it away. It was when she had finished the washing-up that she made an observation.

'It's time you and I came to some sort of an understanding, Walter!'

Cardish looked up absently. 'Is it? Concerning what?'

'The future. Obviously this business of being a seer will mean jail. Either you stop doing it or else make provision for Tommy and me when the blow falls.'

'Many women are notoriously stupid,' Cardish commented, 'and you, my dear, are outstanding in that respect. Will you kindly allow me to handle the affairs of this family and stop talking such non-sense.'

'Jail isn't nonsense!' Bertha's face was becoming shiny. 'It's *bound* to end there! I admit you seem to have some sort of a system which is working all right at the moment but sure enough there'll come a time when you'll go wrong. Then what?'

Cardish sighed and got to his feet. He went over to Bertha and clapped his hands to her ample shoulders.

'Listen, Bertha — and listen carefully. We're only at the very start of a new life. Ahead of us is an infinite supply of money. In a few years there is no reason why I shouldn't become one of the richest men in the world. The law can never touch me because every time I make a forecast it will be a true one. My fame will grow. The trivial cash I brought in today is nothing compared to what will come — It is entirely up to you whether you stay beside me or not. I'm remembering that you are my wife and entitled to share in whatever fortune I may make. I'm also remembering the past years in which you've vilified me in every possible way — '

'Only because you didn't seem to get on Walter! Honest! There wasn't any other reason. It made me mad.'

'Thinking for me, eh?' Cardish's voice was dryly amused.

'Yes. And that's the truth — I'll stay beside you if you're sure there's no danger.'

'Very courageous of you, Bertha! No, there's no danger. But staying beside me entails a condition. You will do exactly as I say and when I wish to be alone you will not disturb me. That understood? The same applies to Tommy.'

'I'll do it,' Bertha promised. 'Will it mean we can have a big house, a decent car, servants, and all that sort of thing?'

'In time.' Cardish studied the round, greasy face from which all traces of youth had everlastingly gone. He sighed and for a moment remembered yesteryear. 'I loved you enough to marry you, Bertha, twenty years ago. Maybe I can recapture something of that — Now I'm going out to sit and think, and don't dare to follow me or ask me where I've been when I come back.'

'No, Walter. Just as you say.'

Cardish nodded, and departed the house. Thereafter he wandered thoughtfully towards the nearest recreation ground, just at the same time as he realised his double was walking along the mighty halls networking the major city of Mazor.

The First in Mathematics was surprised when Walter was shown into his private chambers but he greeted him with that icy reserve habitual to him

'Have I your permission to ask one of my everlasting questions?' Cardish enquired.

'Of course, Earthman. I am always at your service. As I have frequently said, you have so much you can learn.'

Cardish made no comment but sat down as the Mazorian briefly indicated a nearby chair.

'Now, Earthman, I am all attention.'

'Well, sir, it is like this. Suppose I needed a weapon with which to protect myself. What would you suggest?'

'A weapon!' The Mazorian's inscrutable features altered a trifle in expression. 'But why should you require a weapon? Surely there is nobody here whom you fear? We are doing our best to make you feel entirely comfortable.'

'Yes indeed, and you are doing. I don't want you to misunderstand me. I've noticed the many weapons you possess in these laboratories and I've also noticed how lethal they probably are. Just out of idle curiosity I started wondering which of them I'd choose if I had to defend myself.'

'Against what, Earthman?'

'I'm not sure.' Cardish hesitated. 'But I do have the feeling at times that certain members of your race — those who are not in authority as are you and the rest of the 'Firsts' — resent my presence. One of them might think it a good idea to try and kill me one day.'

The Mazorian meditated and Cardish waited to see if his random shot would find a mark. It was sheer bunk about any of the Mazorians resenting his presence, of course. They no more resented him than a human being resents the presence of a worm in the garden — but it was as good a line as any to try out.

'I think,' the First in Mathematics said, rather surprisingly, 'that I know what you mean, Earthman. We of the ruling faction are as much a target for the masses as you are. We because we rule — you because you are alien. Can you specifically indicate which members of the community have behaved inimically towards you?'

'Quite impossible, I'm afraid. All you Mazorians look alike to me. I do hope,' Cardish went on seriously, 'that you appreciate my position? I have nothing but gratitude towards you and the other learned gentlemen, but I am scared of the community in general. That is why I wondered if I could have a weapon with which to protect myself.'

Again the profound reflection. Then: 'I see no reason why not. You are intelligent enough, I think, to know that you cannot possibly get away from this planet and that you would be instantly killed if you dared to wipe out one of our race. I am prepared to grant you some measure of protection, but not with a weapon which can destroy life.'

'What other kind is there?' Cardish asked, puzzled.

'Many kinds. There are weapons that temporarily paralyse an enemy; there are those which blot out memory and therefore make the victim unable to remember the reason for his attack. There are — '

'I like that one,' Cardish broke in eagerly. 'The one that stops memory, I mean. But what happens when memory returns?'

'It doesn't. A permanent state of amnesia is produced. It is not amnesia as you understand it, Earthman. All that is destroyed in the victim's mind is the reason for his attack. He loses no other memories. A very mild but useful means of protection, inflicting no physical harm as such.'

'And would you be willing that I have such a weapon just as a precaution?'

'I would be willing, yes,' the Mazorian assented. 'We of the governing group have instruments about us which give warning when any weapon is about to be used against us, so as far as we are concerned we are immune if you were suddenly prompted to foolish action. As to any other member of our race who might lose his or her control and attack you — well, we would consider the merits or demerits of your case if such an occasion arose. Yes, permission granted.'

Cardish smiled to himself and watched as the mathematician wrote out some details on a card and presently handed it over.

'Take this to the First in Metallurgy,' he instructed. 'You will find your direction in the main hallway. He will then put you in touch with the First in Ballistics. Between them they will provide you with a weapon suitable to your smaller physique, your hands being quite different from ours.'

'Thank you,' Cardish said quietly. 'I'm very grateful.'

He took the card in his hand and began to leave the office. Across the recreation ground the park-keeper came lounging, lighting his pipe slowly.

'Fine evening, sir,' he commented, pausing and surveying the sky; and Cardish nodded.

'Beautiful at the moment. Pity there'll be rain tomorrow.'

'Rain? Bless you, sir, there'll be no rain. I know too much about weather lore to be fooled into thinking that. We're in for a long, dry spell.'

Cardish smiled but said no more, and during the night the rain came. In fact it was so heavy it awakened Cardish out of sleep. He lay listening to it and smiled once again to himself.

By breakfast time the deluge of the night had settled into a steady downpour from all-over grey skies. Tommy, eating his breakfast in gulps as usual, kept looking at his father from under his eyes.

'Looks like you were right, dad,' he admitted finally.

'About the rain?' Cardish eyed him. 'Well, of course I was right. I cannot possibly be wrong — that's the beauty of being an infallible seer.'

'But how do you *do* it, dad?'

'That's my business. Get on with your breakfast.'

Bertha poured out the coffee. 'Business as usual today, Walter?'

'Naturally. Why not?'

'Oh, I just wondered. Think you'll have as good a day as yesterday?'

'Can't see any reason why I shouldn't.

I'll very soon find out.'

This proved to be almost an under-statement. Cardish's first visitor, not five minutes after he had arrived drenched at the office, was a squat, lean-featured man with a dripping mackintosh turned up to his ears. Water ran down his plastered hair as he brushed past the startled Cardish who had just entered the doorway.

'I'm looking for the Great Volta,' the lean-featured man explained. 'Absolutely essential I see him. Where is he? In that office there?'

'He will be presently. Right now you're looking at him.'

'Eh? You! Are *you* the Great Volta? I thought you were the receptionist.'

'Sorry to disappoint you,' Cardish apologised. 'What's the nature of your business?'

'I'm the news editor of the *Daily Flashlight*. You handed me a prediction last night about it raining today and I ran it in this morning's issue. I wish to heaven I'd taken your advice and given it a bigger spread — How the devil did you know this was coming?'

'Just my business,' Cardish smiled.

'This isn't just business, man, it's wizardry! Mind if I make a proposition to you?'

'Not at all. Come into my private office — '

Cardish led the way into it and the editor sat down, a fine semi-circle of water drops collecting round the thick hem of his mackintosh.

'We're always open to anything interesting,' he explained. 'Last night I just took you as a joke — as one usually does these fortune tellers. But you're so damned accurate something ought to be done about it. It really *is* raining all over the country. I've gathered the reports. Our official forecast on the front page says, 'Fine and very warm'. I rang up the weather bureau and they say an unexpected depression developed during the night. Some of the boys there had noticed your own forecast and are wondering how the devil you managed it — Would you consider being the *Flashlight's* official weather man, as apart from the general country-wide meteorological forecast which all the papers print?'

'I might,' Cardish answered, thinking.

'We're willing to take you on for a week. If you get it right for every day you'll become one of the staff. We'll pay three hundred pounds for each daily report. Boost our circulation no end. Well?'

'Fair enough,' Cardish nodded. 'I'll see you get the reports for a week, commencing tomorrow.'

'Tomorrow won't do. I must have tomorrow's report by four o'clock this afternoon. Or is that asking too much?'

'By no means. Precisely at four I'll phone it in to you. And thanks very much.'

The editor did not go. He remained relaxed, studying Cardish's tired face in puzzled interest.

'Don't think me personal, Volta, but you're an odd-looking fellow. Sort of ethereal, if you know what I mean.'

'I know. You mean my general transluscence — A lot of the great visionaries are like that.'

'I suppose you've only just started up in this business?'

'Yes. I never knew I had the gift until recently.'

'How much for an exclusive? Giving the facts of your life and some high-powered predictions thrown in?'

Cardish shook his head. 'I don't want the facts of my life or my real identity, to be publicised. However, I'll compromise on one thing. When I sense something big is going to happen — like a great disaster — I'll see you are the first to know of it. That suit?'

'Fair enough.' The editor got to his feet. 'Anything you can tell me at this moment that might hit the headlines?'

'Not that I know of. Just as a token of thanks though. I would suggest you back Stench of Mystery for the three-thirty this afternoon.

'*That* outsider? Oh, well, if you say so. See you again.'

The editor departed, a man both puzzled and satisfied.

In his long experience of quacks and frauds he had never come across one who seemed so quietly assured of himself. Perhaps he was a Tibetan mystic disguised as an Englishman, or something? Perhaps — Oh, what did it matter, anyway? He had forecast rain and nobody else had. *That* made news.

4

For Cardish this second day was almost a repetition of the first. He had a trickle of clients, many of them wanting advance sporting information, and wherever he could — according to the availability of the Mazorian time-telescope — he supplied the required information. But things did not really begin to happen for him until towards six o'clock when the races were over.

Then, entering like a whirlwind, there came the florid woman of the previous day. Before Cardish had a ghost of a chance she flung her fat arms round his neck and kissed him violently.

'Take no notice of that,' she advised, straightening her rain-sodden hat. 'That's just between friends — a kind of emotional backfire! Mr. Volta, you're a miracle man! Every one of those tips came off. I risked a good deal of money and doubled up. I came off with twenty thousand pounds!'

'Good!' Cardish said, rather nervously.

'Good? Why, it's miraculous!' The florid woman threw her arms wide as though she were going to become airborne. 'Didn't you back those horses yourself?'

'No. Not because I'd any doubts about them but I haven't had time. One long stream of clients — '

'*And* you'll get thousands more, my dear sir! I'll see to that! Maybe you don't know who I am?'

'Well — er — beyond noticing the cheque was signed by Flora Gore-Robinson I'm afraid I have to admit I don't.'

'I, sir, am the wife of Rupert Gore-Robinson, the kettle king! You've heard of Robinson kettles, surely? Boil themselves within seconds like a pressure cooker?'

'No, but it sounds interesting.'

'You shall have one, Mr. Volta, as a gift. I'll see to that! I shall also see that amongst my circle of friends your name is widely publicised. Why, a man with your gifts is unique. Just think of the money you can make for everybody, to say nothing of yourself!'

Cardish nodded. 'Yes, I have been speculating on that pleasant vision.'

'I should think so! Now, what are tomorrow's winners?'

Cardish looked through his files and studied them. 'Quite a lot tomorrow, madam, three meetings. Ten horses. If I may have your post-dated cheque I'll give you the list.'

Flora Gore-Robinson was already scribbling busily in her chequebook, her face tomato-coloured from excitement and muggy weather.

'There you are, Mr. Volta. One thousand pounds — and this time it is *not* post-dated. I have every confidence.'

Cardish smiled and handed over the list. 'I thank you for your trust, madam — and in advance for the pressure-kettle.'

Upon which the wife of the kettle king took her departure and Cardish prepared to return home, this time with £90,000 and a few odd hundreds. Most of it was in cheques and he preferred to put it in a small steel box at home than leave it in the office. When Bertha beheld the total amount lying on the living room table her eyes came out so far it looked as though they would never pop back.

'Of course it can't go on!' she declared. 'This isn't really happening to us Walter. It can't be!'

'It *is* happening, and will continue to do so. Nearly all that money is from that great section of the British public that likes a flutter. The news of an infallible tipster travels fast.'

'So it seems. Why is it you don't ever back any of these horses yourself? Haven't you enough faith in them?'

'I have every faith — but I haven't the time. Tell you what we might do — you back them. Here's tomorrow's list of winners.'

Cardish pulled a sheet from his pocket and put it down. Then he hesitated and picked it up again.

'No,' he said quietly. 'It wouldn't do. You might talk too much. Not you particularly, but *anybody*. That would be bad business. Forget about it. Anyhow, at the rate things are going we hardly need to back horses as well.'

'Maybe you don't because you're making all the money — but I have to be content with what you give me and I don't like it. Please, Walter, just one winner! I won't tell a soul. Honest!'

Cardish hesitated for a long time, then: 'Oh, very well. Put your shirt on Dusty Rump for the two-thirty tomorrow, and not a word to a soul — '

'Can I back it too, dad?'

Cardish turned sharply. He had not noticed that Tommy was lounging in the doorway, a curious grin on his heavy mouth.

'Certainly not! A lad of your age shouldn't need to bet. I won't have it!'

'Why don't you grow up, dad?' Tommy lounged forward. 'The boys all bet, and so do I. This ain't the days of the 'Barretts of Wimpole Street' you know!'

'Nevertheless, I — Oh, very well, back it!' Cardish's face was grim. 'And if you say where the tip came from I'll break your neck.'

Tommy still grinned irritatingly. Cardish turned and looked at Bertha.

'I've a phone call to make, Bertha. Fix my meal up meantime.' He went to the hall telephone, and got through to the news editor of the *Flashlight*.

'Sorry, I forgot the four o'clock deadline for the weather forecast,' Cardish apologised. 'I've been very busy.'

'I don't wonder if all your tips are as good as the one you gave me. I'm two hundred quid richer so I'll forgive you missing the deadline. I can still make it somehow. Well, what's the weather to be?'

'Fine in the south and east, thunder showers in the north and west. I'm not smart enough to guess what the temperature will be, but there you have the kind of day.'

'Good enough, and it's in conflict again with the meteorological office! They're going to love you in a bit Volta! Incidentally I'm running these forecasts under the headline of 'Volta Predicts' if that's okay?'

'Quite.'

'Then if anything big turns up that can also go into the same column. Believe me, you'll be famous in no time.'

'I'll be on time with tomorrow's forecast,' Cardish promised. ' 'Bye for now.'

He returned to the kitchen to find that his and Bertha's meal was laid out in readiness. Tommy's had vanished and so had Tommy. As usual he had bolted everything in sight and then departed to his sub-human companions.

'I have decided,' Cardish said, with the air of a governing director, 'to buy a house. A large one, completely detached, and with every modern convenience — and talking of convenience, a pressure-kettle will be coming along soon. From a grateful client.'

'Oh,' Bertha said, eating stew a trifle noisily. 'Where is this new house to be?'

'I'd thought of *Daisy Bank*, just down the road from here.'

Bertha chewed and stared simultaneously. 'That place must be worth a fortune! Why, it used to be a nursing home.'

'The price is pretty hefty, but we can afford it now. As well as the costs of bringing the place up to date.'

'Yes,' Bertha admitted vaguely. 'I suppose so — '

'Added to which there'll be incidentals,' Cardish continued, musing. 'Housekeeper, servants, gardeners, a chauffeur. I should think two Rolls-Royces will do for a start for official business, and if you need a little runabout just let me know.'

'Fantastic,' Bertha whispered. 'That's what it is! And where does Tommy come into all this?'

'Tommy,' Cardish said deliberately, 'will go to college and have the hard corners knocked off him. Get him away from those wide boys he spends his time with — to say nothing of quite a gang of doubtful young women. Oh, yes, my dear, there are going to be quite a few changes. Take a bit of time, of course, but at the rate the money's coming in another month should see me in the position to make a big move.'

Bertha nodded, which seemed quite the safest thing to do — and Cardish said no more until the meal was over then a thought seemed to strike him.

'I've more telephoning to do. I need to

contact the managing director of a reliable firm of precision-instrument makers.'

'Precision instruments? *Now* what?'

'A special weapon, m'dear. Never mind why.'

Cardish rose and went to the telephone. Eventually he was able to get in touch with the private residence of Brandon J. Kellog, director of the Peak Precision Engineering Company. Apparently the great man was at home.

'You will not know me,' Cardish said. 'My business name is 'Volta' and I am a prognosticator of future events.'

'Uh-huh,' commented the gravel voice at the other end.

'I need a specially made gun drawn entirely to my own specifications. There's nothing like it anywhere in this world, so you have no precedent. Would you be willing to take on the job?'

'Gun? What sort of a gun? Big thing?'

'Not very. About the size of an ordinary thirty-five but with an extremely large and specially-made firing mechanism where the butt ordinarily is.'

'Don't think I can do it, Mr. Volta.

We're under exclusive contract to the War Ministry and if we turn out a gun which is not vetted by the Government there may be trouble.'

'Be damned to the War Ministry! This is a private transaction and I'll pay any reasonable sum to have the gun made.'

Silence, indicative of reflection at the other end. Then: 'Sorry, Mr. Volta. I'd like to help you, but without any official authority on your part — Well, you know how it is.'

'Supposing I had the authority of the Society for Physical Research?'

'Ah! Now there you would have something.'

'Right!' Cardish exclaimed. 'I'll get in touch with you again, sir — and thanks.'

He rang off, searched the directory for Dr. Gascoyne's home number — found so many Gascoynes he did not know which to pick — and left his home with some impatience. Half an hour later he was in Kensington, and fifteen minutes after that he was entering the doors of the Society for Physical Research, which were still open. From the look of the many lighted windows from the outside, gleaming obscurely in the misty summer evening, it looked as if the place was at work twenty-four hours a day.

Cardish found himself directed by one white-coated assistant after another until he finally landed in an anteroom. Into here there presently bobbed the pink-cheeked chubby Dr. Gascoyne, an acid-stained smock thrown over his suit.

'Well, well, Cardish — glad to see you.' He shook hands vigorously. 'You're lucky, you know. I usually leave around six, but this time something special had to be done. Now, what's on your mind?'

'I merely want you to handle a job for me. It has to have the backing of an organisation like this. The firm is Peak Precision Engineering.'

'Yes. I know them.' Gascoyne sat down. 'And what's the job?'

'A Mazorian gun. I've got all the details — from none other than the First in Mathematics himself. He demurred a bit but finally gave me the facts.'

'A gun, eh?' Gascoyne looked surprised. 'Am I entitled to ask why?'

'It's for my own protection.' Cardish looked serious. 'Between ourselves, Gascoyne, ever since this double effect came into being, I have become oddly psychic. I can sort of feel when danger's coming and for some time now I've been haunted by the conviction that danger is coming to me. I have no idea from what source, but I mean to be ready for it when it happens. Hence the gun.'

'I see. Quite understandable. What sort of a gun is it?'

'Quite an amazing one. It destroys the memory of a certain intention. For instance, if you wanted to murder me and I turned the gun on you you'd forget what you wanted to do to me; but you wouldn't forget anything else. Sort of local amnesia producer.'

'Mmmm.' Gascoyne thought for a moment. 'That sounds like a masterpiece. Be a useful addition to our defences, too, and — '

'No!' Cardish shook his head. 'This has nothing to do with our defences. It is entirely for *me*, and you are the one to handle it,' and he added the details of his brief phone conversation with P.P.E.'s managing director.

'Okay.' Gascoyne smiled. 'What are the details? I'll see what I can do.'

It was also about this time that somebody else was asking for details — of a very different nature. Tommy Cardish, in fact, surrounded by about half a dozen of his scrub-headed, wide-jacketed contemporaries was doing his best to look mysterious and not succeeding very well.

'Come off it, Tommy!' one of the youths jeered. 'Your old man can't pick horses out of the air just like that! He must have either inside information or be in touch with a mighty good tipster.'

'He hasn't neither!' Tommy shouted, his lips jutting. 'I tell you he's a seer! Ain't you never heard of the Great Volta? My old man can predict anything! Just *anything*! An' if he says 'Dusty Rump' is going t'win tomorrow, it will!'

'Great Volta!' sneered another. 'Blimey, some name! Why don't he stick to his own monicker?'

'I dunno. I s'pose he just thinks 'Volta' sounds more impressive. But it's honest, fellers. He really can see things afore they happen. Take t'day, frinstance. He said it was going to be wet and all the forecasts said fine. He was right, wasn't he?'

'Certainly was wet,' one of the gang agreed. 'But whether your pop said it would be we don't know. I think you're just gaggin', Tommy, an — '

'I'm *not* gagging! You wait until 'Dusty Rump' wins tomorrow. Then you'll see! An' he can pick any horse anywhere, any time — just like that! There's a fortune in it!'

'For him, mebbe,' another commented. 'Mighty rough on the bookies, though, My dad wouldn't like it a bit.'

Tommy's expression changed. He had overlooked for the moment that one of the gang was Cliff Naylor, son of a somewhat doubtful bookmaker.

'Look, there's to be no telling of anybody what I've told you!' Tommy insisted. 'That agreed? I've only told you as much as I have because you're my pals. Ain't no need for you to go bleatin' it to everybody!'

''Ark at him,' Cliff Naylor grinned. 'His old man's a seer and can't miss and he don't want anybody to know about it! What kind of talk is that?'

That Tommy was worried from that moment onward could not be denied, but of course he said nothing at home. And the following day Dusty Rump romped home in spite of all the punters' forecasts to the contrary. Bookmakers who had clients who were also Cardish's clients had the roughest time in years . . . And Walter Cardish smiled, mentally controlled his other self to make a survey through the Mazorian time-telescope, and once more supplied his increasing band of callers with infallible tips.

Strangely enough, as Bertha had once remarked, this couldn't go on! After a fortnight of infallible tips and flawless weather reports Volta was commencing to hit the front page. The directors of the turf associations held extraordinary meetings to decide what ought to be done about this mystery man who was never wrong and who never went near a racecourse. But that was the point — nothing *could* be done. There exists in law no penalty for a man or woman who can accurately foretell the future, and by this decision the bookmakers had to abide — the honest-to-God ones anyhow. Others were less passive — as Cardish one morning discovered.

It was a month after he had established himself. Half way through the morning a different type of client came into the office, brushing past the newly-employed and highly delectable red-headed secretary and barging straight into Cardish's office. He glanced up from his desk, immediately scenting danger through that odd psychic instinct he seemed lately to have developed.

'You Volta?' demanded the newcomer.

'I am.' Cardish's voice was quiet. 'Sit down, my friend.'

'I won't sit down, and I'm not your friend! The name's Naylor. Mebbe you've heard of me — your Tommy goes round with my boy Cliff.'

'Does he now? I'm afraid I've little interest in what my son does. He goes his own way.'

'I don't blame him with you for a father — cheatin' honest men out of a living.'

Cardish raised an eyebrow. The premonition of trouble was still with him. Naylor was a big, powerful man, looking all the bigger in the vulgar check suit he was wearing. He had a florid face, baggy cheeks, and very inflamed grey eyes.

'Out with it,' Cardish said finally. 'What's on your mind?'

'You are, and your damned betting forecasts! Do you know how much I've had to pay out this past month? Near on a hundred thousand pounds! Not all of it mine, neither — I've had to borrow. If it goes on I'll be out of business. So will every damned bookmaker in the country.'

'Well?'

'Don't sit there and say 'Well?' to me!' Naylor roared. 'It's got to stop, and if it doesn't, Mr. Knowall, I'm warning you that there'll be a new face for Saint Peter to look at — and damned soon!'

Cardish smiled. Naylor's red face changed to a deep purple.

'It's nothing to blasted well grin at!' he bellowed.

'That depends.' Cardish sat back comfortably in his chair. 'I am not smiling at your misfortune, my friend, but at the colossal nerve you must have to order me to stop forecasting just because it pinches your pocket. You know your remedy if it hurts that much. Simply refuse to accept clients who are also *my* clients.'

'What! And lose thousands?'

'Not necessarily. You must have quite a lot of clients who don't deal with me. Make your money out of their losses and don't come bothering me again. If you do I'll find a legal way to have you put under restraint.'

'Why, you damned — '

'I am running a perfectly honest business,' Cardish snapped, his tone changing. 'It can stand investigation by any authority in the land. Can you say the same about your business?'

Naylor clenched his fists. 'You're not going to get away with this, Volta. By hell you're not! You'll see!'

He swung, snatched the door open, and charged outside. The door slammed shut violently. Cardish thought for a moment and then picked up the telephone. In a moment or two he was talking to Gascoyne.

'Better ginger them up with that Mazorian gun,' he said briefly. 'I think the trouble I scented is on its way.'

'Why? What's happened?'

Cardish explained.

'Tell the police,' Gascoyne said. 'Naylor can't come barging into your place threatening what he'll do. There are laws against it.'

'I know that, but I'd start getting my name in the papers, and probably on the TV and radio. My own name, I mean, and I don't want the Mazorians to pick it up. I'll handle this myself, providing I get that gun quickly.'

'I'll see to it. Can't blame the engineers for the delay, though — they're having to work on a mighty tricky instrument.'

Cardish rang off and glanced up as the red-head knocked and came in.

'A Mr. Donaldson, sir, of the Meteorological Department.'

'Oh!' Cardish sighed. 'Right, Miss Drew. Have him come in, please.'

The tall, bald-headed meteorologist entered quickly, gave a brief nod, shook hands and sat down.

'I am here on official business, Mr. — er — Volta.'

'I've been expecting it. I suppose you've come to upbraid me for having made hay of your weather forecasts?'

'Anything but it! On the contrary we at the meterological bureau envy your startling accuracy. Not unnaturally we have been called to account by various aircraft and shipping bodies for not tallying with *your* forecast, which is always correct. You understand, sir, that a body as important as the Weather Bureau cannot keep on being held up to ridicule.'

'The alternative is simple. Mr. — er —?'

'Donaldson, Mr. Volta. I am the head meteorologist of the London weather centre.'

'Ah! Well, as I said, your alternative is simple. Get your forecasts *right* and there'll be no trouble.'

'We get them as right as we can. This country is a weather forecaster's night-mare, as you must realise.'

'I suppose so, yes. Am I to understand

that, in a round-about way, you are asking *me* to stop forecasting?'

Hope came to the thin man's face, and faded on the next words.

'Sorry, Mr. Donaldson, but it can't be done. I'm under contract to the *Daily Flashlight* to forecast the weather for the next ten years.'

'We would be willing to buy up that contract.'

Cardish shrugged. 'Up to you. Nothing I can do about it. To be candid, I can't see what you're so worried about.'

'It's the prestige of the thing, my dear sir! We are looked to for accurate reports, near as we can give them — then you, without any instruments, weather stations, or any material aid whatsoever, say exactly what is going to happen and make most of us look a lot of imbeciles. Aircraft corporations and shipping lines are taking far more notice of you these days than us — Do you want to put us all out of work?'

Cardish sighed. 'Certainly I don't — but I have my contract to live up to, unless you buy it up. I'm sorry, Mr.

Donaldson, but there's nothing I can do.'

The meteorologist rose. 'Thank you for seeing me,' he said politely, but he departed with a certain look of threat in his eyes, which, for the time being anyway, seemed to end the visits of those who objected to the Great Volta's uncanny accuracy. For the rest of the day Cardish found himself kept busy with quite legitimate clients, and the day after that and the day after that.

When he was not at the office he spent his time supervising the change in his domestic life. He, Bertha and Tommy had already moved into *Daisy Bank*, and by day joiners and builders making the renovations nearly drove Bertha crazy with their noise and confusion. Between them and the ultra rapid pressure kettle that boiled water in seconds she seemed to have been suddenly pitched into a world where everything moved at top speed — a most disturbing condition to one with a slow-motion mind like herself.

Tommy, soundly censured for giving the son of Naylor the 'low down', had already been told he would shortly leave for college, and that in the meantime his association with the 'gang' must cease. So didactic had his father become he did not even think of disobeying . . .

For the rest there was the wooden-faced chauffeur-handyman, the domestic staff, and the dozen and one details that Bertha had not the wit to handle. Altogether, Cardish had his hands full, and all the time he was conscious of the amazing gift that had been wished upon him. There was nothing to stop him making untold millions simply because he could see further than any other human being on Earth. The position was unique, and yet it carried a secret dread of which he never spoke. He knew that, logically, it must end somewhere, and now and again he spent a morbid hour trying to find out where his own adventure would end. He could not discover it. He knew there ought to be some sign of it, but evidently through the Mazorian time-telescope he had not happened to alight on the vital moment.

So his fame spread, but on no account would he allow his own name to be published, and in every case he refused to be interviewed by television. His queer vetoes were taken as indication of his strange genius and duly respected.

Then one late September evening he ran into the trouble he had sensed was coming. Delayed at the office preparing for next day he did not leave until nearly eleven o'clock. The car was waiting for him as usual, the wooden-faced chauffeur respectful and silent — seeming even more taut than usual.

'Feeling unwell, Danvers?' Cardish asked him, surprised.

'I'm quite well, sir, thank you.' The chauffeur hesitated as though he wanted to say something, but checked himself.

In another moment Cardish knew the reason for his queer behaviour. There were two men in the back of the limousine, and Cardish found himself sitting beside them before he could make a move. The deep twilight and extinguished roof light had given them the advantage, and evidently the chauffeur had been covered with a gun also, hence his reticence.

'Your chauffeur,' said bookmaker Naylor bitterly, 'knows exactly what he has to do, and he also knows he'll get a bullet in his neck if he doesn't. You're going for a ride, Mr. Volta Cardish. I warned you some time ago to stop monkeying around with racing tips, but you took no notice.'

'Nor shall I,' Cardish answered, as the car started moving.

'I wouldn't be too confident of that. I'm not just acting for myself in this — I'm acting for all of us who've taken the devil's own beating because of your tips. You're going to quietly disappear, Mr. Cardish, like the rest of people who know more than's good for 'em.'

Cardish made no answer. He had in his overcoat pocket the Mazorian gun. It had been there for a fortnight now. He never went anywhere outside without it. In the same pocket was a handkerchief. He withdrew the handkerchief and dabbed his lips, but when he returned the handkerchief to his pocket he kept his hand there — ready.

'Starting to sweat a bit?' the bookmaker asked cynically. 'Good! Now you know

117

how we boys have felt when we've seen our money just vanishing from under our noses. All 'cos of you, Mr. Knowall!'

'This other man in with you?' Cardish asked, glancing.

'Yes,' the other man growled. 'I've been cleaned out, with a lot of the other boys.'

'Which must make the bookmaking business a lot sweeter,' Cardish commented, and ignoring the smothered fury of his unwanted companions he gazed through the window.

Following out instructions Danvers was driving swiftly away from the busy streets of the metropolis, twisting and twining down alleyways and side streets. Eventually he reached the area of the docks, and at the corner of a dim, deserted street.

'Out!' Naylor snapped. 'And don't forget my gun's loaded.'

Cardish shrugged and one-handed opened the door and alighted. He stood waiting as his chauffeur was bundled beside him, then Naylor glanced around him in the gloom.

'All right — start walking. The river's at the end of this street and the way it'll look you two will be accidentally drowned.'

Cardish made no response and Danvers gave him a taut anxious glance. Danvers was not a big man, otherwise he would no doubt have made a final effort to save himself. Instead he walked beside his employer and as they walked the sound of the lapping river waters came ever nearer. Far away in the still September night a tug hooted dismally.

'May I say something?' Cardish asked, pausing.

'Well?' Naylor squared up in front of him, his gun ready.

'Just this — '

Cardish kicked his right foot with all his strength, the sharp toe of his shoe cutting deep into Naylor's shinbone. It was quite a simple action unseen in the dark and equally unexpected.

There is not a man living who can take a vicious kick on the shin and remain unmoved — and Naylor was no exception. He gave a gasp of anguish and hopped abruptly. Instantly Cardish slammed up his right fist. Excitement gave him more strength than he normally had and the blow sent the bookmaker spinning to the tarry boards of the wharf.

The second man grasped the details in a split second and fired his gun, just at the instant that the chauffeur knocked his arm up. The bullet went skywards and a stinging punch straight in the stomach doubled the second man up like a pen-knife. The chauffeur retracted his fist for a second blow but Cardish stopped him.

'No need for fisticuffs, Danvers. Everything should be under control from here on.'

Danvers looked apprehensive, and hovered on the verge of making a dash for it: then he frowned as Cardish pulled a queer little gun from his pocket. It glittered dully in the dim street lamps, a curious metallic bag hanging from the butt. Cardish aimed it first at the bookmaker, pressing a concealed button; then at the second man. Nothing apparently happened. There was no beam, no sound, and the men seemed unhurt. They got up slowly, breathing hard.

Cardish waited, trying to keep his nervousness controlled. Danvers looked warily at the two automatics nearby.

'That's funny,' Naylor said, scratching his bullet head. 'Something here I don't get. You two fellers know anything about it?'

'About what?' Cardish asked politely.

'What I'm doing here. Why, I was lying there — Hell, my jaw! Feel as though something hit me. Hey, Joe! How'd we get here?'

'No idea,' the second man said.

There was silence; Danvers stared blankly whilst Cardish waited for the next.

'I sort of remember coming here,' Joe said, scratching the back of his neck, 'but that's all I do remember! It just doesn't make sense — '

'Probably the pub down the road can explain it.' Cardish observed, pocketing his weapon before either man had a chance to glimpse it. 'My chauffeur and I heard you arguing and thought perhaps a suicide was contemplated, so we came to look. If you're wise, boys, you'll go home and sleep it off. You must have been fighting.'

'Yes,' Naylor muttered ruefully. 'That's about the size of it, mister.'

Cardish jerked his head and he and Danvers went back towards the car. The chauffeur's face was a study in the dim street lighting.

'Don't let it upset you, Danvers,' Cardish remarked dryly. 'There's a perfectly logical reason for what happened, though I don't intend to explain it. Let's get back home whilst we're safe.'

'Yes, sir. Right away.'

5

Walter Cardish drifted silently down the great corridors of the Mazorian laboratories. It was the end of the rest period when the Mazorians resumed their normal 'daily' work. And as usual, having breakfasted comfortably — on food specially prepared for him — Cardish finished his journey in the big laboratory where the time-telescope was housed, to commence his usual survey of Earth 24 hours ahead in Time.

For a long time he did not behold anything of outstanding importance. He read the raceboards at the usual meetings and then controlled the giant instrument so that it tracked at close quarters up and down England in the brilliantly sunny autumn day. Nothing unexpected. The usual green fields — a little brown now — the winding lanes, the villages, a streak of motion from an advancing express train . . .

No, two streaks of motion, moving in opposite directions towards each other, separated by perhaps ten miles. Cardish frowned, suddenly finding his pulses racing. He quickly adjusted the focussing mechanism and watched enthralled, even fascinated by horror, as he realised both trains were flying towards each other at a mile and more a minute.

He cried out sharply, oblivious to the incomprehensible barrier of Time and space separating him from Earth.

The disaster came. The two trains converged in one mighty belch of flame and smoke. Carriages reared into the air others bounced and bounded down the embankments. Flame began to javelin through broken windows and torn wood-work. Bodies lay smashed and dead in the midst of twisted steelwork.

'My God!' Cardish whispered, perspiration streaming down his face. 'Oh, my God — '

With a shaking hand he twisted the fine-focus screw, which gave him the ultimate in magnification. He swept the lens over the tangled wreckage until he located one listing carriage with a board on it. CREWE — LONDON. This done he looked at the master-clock that gave the exact time on Earth as the telescope viewed it — a refinement Cardish had especially requested to be installed on his personal switchboard. It was 3.16 precisely, and obviously post-meridian. Still keeping things under control Cardish swung the telescope again, its hair tracking device enabling it to creep gradually over the Earth landscape despite the enormous distance.

He came eventually to a station, the last one through which the Crewe — London express had passed. A pretty, flower-decked little place with the station name of Kelland Upthorn . . . Breathing hard, Cardish switched off the mechanism and sat trying to control his emotions.

'Something troubling you, Earthman?'

Cardish looked up with a start. The tall, impersonal First in Mathematics was close behind him, hands locked — as was his custom — at his back.

'I — I just saw a railway accident back

home and it sort of — sort of jolted me. Horrible sight!'

'I cannot understand your emotion, Earthman. Why be affected by something happening on a planet you will never tread again?'

'It's not that. Those poor people I saw are fellow beings of mine. Earth people. There's a kinship — Or don't you understand what I mean?'

The bald dome shook slowly. 'No, Earthman. I do not understand what you mean. We of this world are entirely sufficient unto ourselves and do not saddle ourselves with sentiment towards others. You would be happier if you cultivated a similar attitude.'

'I can't.' Cardish got up slowly from before the instrument. 'Earth people have feelings, sentiments, and I'm no exception.'

There was a long silence. The mathematician seemed to be thinking something out. Whatever it was he did not refer to it — instead he turned to one of the computers and set it in operation, evidently the reason for his visit to the laboratory. Cardish watched him moodily for a time and then went out into the hallways . . .

And during breakfast at home he was looking taut and strained, so much so that Bertha could not help but notice it.

'What's the matter?' she asked bluntly.

'Nothing you'd understand, Bertha. Just keep quiet and let me think.'

'Nothing going wrong with the seer business, is there? I'm expecting to hear of it any day.'

'No, there *isn't* anything wrong with the seer business. In fact that's just the trouble. I've seen something dreadful and I think it's up to me to issue a warning. The Crewe-London express is going to be wrecked today at three-sixteen. It's absolutely inevitable. I can't just stand by and let it happen.'

Bertha frowned. 'If it's inevitable you can't do anything about it, can you?'

Such logic from Bertha was too much. And there was the vacant, wondering stare of Tommy, too. Cardish finished his breakfast in morose silence and then departed for his office, glancing through the newspaper whilst Danvers drove the limousine. Cardish half had the idea that the escapade of the night before might have found its way into the papers, but there was no mention of it. Evidently the memory-destroying weapon was all that the First in Mathematics claimed for it, or else Naylor preferred to keep quiet and let the matter drop.

But this train smash which was to come! That was the dreadful thing — and it also put Cardish in a difficult spot. He would be compelled to come into the open to explain himself and why he knew it would happen. If he didn't explain himself nobody would believe him anyway. Then again, he had seen many dozens of men and women killed and maimed which meant, no matter what happened, that they would be killed and maimed. Nothing could alter Time.

'Oh, hell,' Cardish muttered, and finally he gave directions to Danvers to head for Kensington and the Physical Research Bureau, this was a matter which needed discussing with a proven friend — and that was what Gascoyne appeared to be so far. He listened with his usual thoughtful silence as Cardish gave him the details, then finally he pursed his lips.

'Nothing else for it, old man, you'll have to give warning,' he said frankly. 'This is a business which outweighs all personal considerations. You owe it to your conscience.'

'That's true enough, and I want to do the honest thing — but when afterwards it comes out, as it will, that I forecast the accident my name is bound to be mentioned. My own name, I mean. And the radio and TV will doubtless give it in the news bulletins.'

'You can demand that only the name of Volta be used. That request will be respected, I'm sure. There's another side to this too, remember. Terrific publicity! Let your editor friend have the details right away. He ought to be able to splash things.'

'In his paper?' Cardish gave a moody glance. 'Wouldn't be any use. Today's issue is finished with and tomorrow will be too late.'

'Give him the particulars anyway. He's a newspaper man and he'll know what to do with this business.'

So, reluctantly, Cardish accepted the suggestion. He left the Research building and made a personal visit to the *Flashlight* offices.

'And there's no doubt in your mind about this?' the editor asked finally.

'No doubt whatever I know it's the Crewe-London express and I know the accident will happen at three-sixteen, but which train it is exactly I can't say.'

'Soon find out.' The editor reached to the phone. 'Euston will tell us.'

He spent several minutes getting details from the Euston stationmaster and then put the phone down again. His face was troubled.

'It'll be the two-forty from Crewe,' he announced. 'It goes through Kelland-Upthorn just after three-twelve. That's the one all right. Only one thing I can do about-it — use my privilege as an editor and as the exclusive publisher of your forecasts to have the B.B.C. put out a warning announcement. It may do good — it may not. Agreed?'

'No other way,' Cardish admitted, sighing.

The editor wasted no more time. He contacted the B.B.C. and afterwards spent the best part of half an hour getting to the right person. Even then there was demur. Oh, yes, the Great Volta had been heard of and his predictions were undoubtedly interesting, but *really* — ! To predict that the Crewe-London express would be wrecked at three-sixteen was absurd. No human being could be *that* accurate. Maybe he could foresee a wreck but not the precise time of it, surely? He could? Oh, very well if only for conscience's sake an emergency warning would be put out. Yes, immediately.

'All I can do,' the editor said, as he explained things to Cardish. 'That's the limit, as far as I'm concerned. Believe me. I'll give you the biggest build-up ever over this.'

'Suppressing my own name, I hope.' Cardish rose from his chair, his eyes troubled.

'Yes, if you want it that way. Either you're damned modest or absolutely crazy. I've never understood which.'

'The Great Volta is enough for me.

That's the name I want to boost. Walter Cardish just wouldn't mean anything.'

'Right!' The editor turned back to his work and Cardish went on his way to the office. Here, somewhat to the surprise of his receptionist-secretary, he switched on the portable radio and sat listening to it turned down whilst he dealt with his clients. Perhaps he missed something in trying to divide his attention, but he was prepared to swear by lunch hour that the B.B.C. had not kept its word.

Promptly he rang up the *Flashlight*. The news editor sounded glum.

'No, you didn't miss anything, Cardish,' he responded. 'The B.B.C. enquired first from the Railway Executive if they had any objection to the broadcast, and it seems they certainly had! They vowed legal action if such a warning was broadcast. Complained it would cut their returns, frighten people away, and Lord knows what — '

'But you don't mean they're not *going* to give warning!' Cardish gasped.

'That's it. No use flying off the handle, old man. We've done all we can. Needless to say, if there *is* an accident this newspaper will blast the B.B.C. and the railway executive wide open — '

'If!' Cardish cried. 'There's no doubt about it! All right, I'll have to try something on my own account.'

At that moment he had not the least idea what. Having failed to budge officialdom in the slightest he could see nothing else for it but his personal intervention. But where? Certainly they wouldn't listen to him at Crewe even if he could get there in time. It was half-past twelve now and the train left at twenty to three. No, that wasn't it.

There was perhaps another way. Get to the signal-box near Kelland-Upthorn and try and have the signalman give warning. That might do it.

'It won't you know,' a little voice insisted to Cardish, as he thought desperately. 'You have *seen* that accident and you cannot possibly stop something which is recorded in Time as happening. It is as impossible as expecting a photograph already taken to mysteriously disappear!'

'But I've got to try,' Cardish whispered. 'Dammit. I've *got* to!'

He wasted no more time. He chartered a plane to Leicester, the nearest point, as it seemed to him, from which to make a dash to Kelland-Upthorn. The matter of the plane settled he made contact with Leicester airport and finally secured the promise of a fast car to meet his plane and afterwards convey him wherever he directed. That left just time to get lunch and then depart.

'I shan't be back until tomorrow, Miss Gadshaw,' Cardish explained to his receptionist. 'I think the most important clients have been dealt with, as far as the racing is concerned. Other prognostications must wait — Oh, you might advise the *Flashlight* before four o'clock that tomorrow's weather will be similar to today. Fine but cold.'

'Yes, sir. I'll lock up and leave at the usual time. If there should be any enquiry from your home, am I to say where you have gone?'

'I'm bound for Leicester. Most important business.'

And Cardish departed, leaving Miss Gadshaw with the private thought that she could probably leave half an hour earlier than usual and so have a longer evening with the boy friend . . .

★   ★   ★

Just after six o'clock that evening, as he was preparing to leave the laboratories, Gascoyne was surprised to have an assistant announcing that Mr. Cardish wished to see him. He hurried out of his overall and went into the anteroom, then paused in surprise. Cardish was sitting in a chair, his head in his hands, his whole attitude one of profound dejection.

'What the devil — ?' Gascoyne moved forward quickly. 'Cardish! What's wrong?'

'Everything!' Cardish looked up, his face haggard. 'I felt I had to tell somebody and you seemed about the only person who'd really understand. I didn't save the express.'

'Surely you didn't expect to do so personally?'

Cardish dragged a newspaper from his

pocket and threw it down. It was copy of the *Evening Gazette*. The front page headline read:

EXPRESS WRECKED!
177 DEAD! 43 INJURED!

Followed by the usual photographs and columns of description.

'I tried to stop the train,' Cardish muttered. 'I flew to Leicester, took a fast car to Kelland-Upthorn, where I thought I might somehow stop the express even if I had to overpower the signalman if he didn't listen to me — Only it didn't work out. The car blew a tyre four miles from the spot and I was too late to act. I would have attempted it only all other means failed.'

'Other means?'

'I tried everything. The editor, the B.B.C. — The public *could* have been warned but for the Railway Executive taking a dim view of the proceedings. So there it is.' Cardish sighed. 'Somehow I feel personally responsible.'

'No reason why you should. You've

done all you can — You should have known that nothing could avert the smash. You saw it in future Time and Time is always correct.'

'I know, but I felt I might have saved a few — Well, that's that! Tomorrow, though, I'm going to be flung into the limelight good and hard. The *Flashlight* editor said he'd raise hell because my warning was ignored. I may need you as a standby.'

'Only too glad. Personally I think you're taking this thing the wrong way. Sorry though I am for the poor folks who were in this smash, it is tremendous publicity for the Great Volta.'

There was no doubt about that, as Cardish discovered the following morning when he opened the *Flashlight*. The headlines came out and hit him:

CREWE-LONDON SMASH NEEDLESS! THE GREAT VOLTA GAVE WARNING!

This paper unreservedly believes that the disastrous railway accident of yesterday need not have happened had not officialdom stepped in and prevented the broadcasting of a warning given by the Great Volta, Prognosticator Extraordinary. Thousands of people can testify to the accuracy of Volta's predictions in the field of gambling and weather forecasting, and we know that he foresaw the exact time of the Crewe-London disaster and tried to have the B.B.C. issue a special warning. The Railway Executive is entirely responsible for the warning not being given, and this paper will press for a public enquiry at the highest level.

There was a good deal more, too, but Cardish's main concern was to discover if his name was mentioned anywhere. It was not. The editor had kept his word.

'If this doesn't put you on top, nothing will,' Bertha commented, as Cardish handed her the paper. 'As for you going all moody because of the dead and injured, I think that's silly. I'm as sorry for them as you are of course, but what's happened has happened and that's all there is to it.'

'Railways apart,' Tommy said, 'what's the best bet for today, dad?'

Cardish gave him a sharp glance. 'You'll get no more tips from me, my boy. You don't know how to keep your mouth shut afterwards.'

'Oh, have a heart, dad! It's bad enough having nothing to do during the summer holidays without being held out from sure-fire racing tips as well! The more I make out of your tips the less I have to come on you for pocket-money.'

'Very logical, my boy, but you're still not getting anything more out of me. Thanks to you talking too much I nearly lost my life a night or so ago at the hands of a thug bookmaker called Naylor. I didn't give you the details before but there they are! Anyway, when you go to college there'll be an end to all this conniving with the mob.'

Tommy made a grimace and said no more. Neither for that matter did Cardish. He finished breakfast, made a final round of the various workmen still improving the residence, and then he was driven to the office. To his surprise he found two clients already waiting for him, though why the delectable Miss Gadshaw was looking vaguely scared he could not quite understand.

'Be with you in a moment, gentlemen,' he said, opening his private office door. 'I don't usually get clients much before ten.'

The two men did not say anything. They were tall, square-shouldered, austere fellows, attired in dark blue lounge suits and carrying mackintoshes on their arms. There was something about them that Cardish felt was vaguely familiar, but he could not pin it down. He felt too that psychic sense of warning which so often assailed him when danger was threatening.

'Now, gentlemen — ' He closed the private door and motioned to chairs. 'What can I do for you?'

The man with the squarest face withdrew something from his inner pocket and held it forward. Clearly it was a warrant card issued by the Metropolitan Police. Cardish had time to see the ominous prefix 'Chief Inspector', and then the card closed again.

'I'm a police officer, Mr. Cardish,' the chief inspector explained. 'Chief Inspector Vincent, Railways Division.'

'I see,' Cardish said quietly, his eyes jumping to the second man.

'And Detective-Sergeant Mason,' Vincent added. 'If you don't mind, sir, I'd like to ask you a few questions.'

'Professional or personal?'

'Possibly both. I understand you have the business name of the Great Volta, and that your real name is Walter Cardish?'

'Correct. I noticed you mentioned my name before. Who gave it to you?'

'The editor of the *Flashlight*. Possibly you are now mentally blaming him for doing that, but I can assure you he had no choice. I had to know all about you.'

'What the devil for?' Cardish demanded. 'I'm running a perfectly honest business here.'

'We are not concerned with that, sir. What we are concerned with is the wreck of the Crewe-London express.'

Cardish looked astonished. 'But why come to me?'

The chief inspector cleared his throat and took a copy of the *Flashlight* from his pocket.

'According to this, sir, and to the editor himself, you — er — foresaw the accident to the Crewe express and tried to give warning.'

'That is so, yes. But for official bungling there wouldn't have been an accident!'

'We have reason to think, Mr. Cardish, that you knew very well that your warning would not be heeded and therefore, to make your apparent prediction come true, you were not unconnected with the accident.'

Cardish frowned. 'Have you the damned temerity to sit there and accuse me of wrecking the express? Is that it?'

'Let us put it this way,' the chief inspector said patiently. 'First, you gave a warning to a newspaper which has consistently published your 'predictions'. Either by luck or some system of your own your predictions have so far been accurate. But to catch the public eye you needed something big — say a railway smash. If a train smash were predicted by you, and came true, what a triumph for you! If on the other hand your warning were heeded and the Crewe express was taken off, what a triumph! Either way you stood to win public acclaim. Rightly, the Railway Executive was not to be bamboozled by any such clairvoyant rubbish, and the train went in the usual way — and was wrecked! Your prediction came true — '

Cardish was silent, his face grim.

'You knew that this morning your prediction would be in the *Flashlight*. You knew that if no accident had happened your professional career would be at an end. It *had* to happen ... Many members of the public are aware of your rise to prominence as a so-called seer, and no doubt you are making plenty out of it. I repeat, a failure would break you.'

'I never heard such a crazy theory in all my life,' Cardish declared levelly.

'The police, Mr. Cardish, are not in the

habit of making statements without proving their worth to begin with. I understand you chartered a plane to Leicester yesterday the moment you had been informed by the *Flashlight* editor that your warning was not going to be published?'

'Well — er — Yes, I did.'

'We know you did, sir. You had a fast car waiting for you with instructions to bead for Kelland-Upthorn, quite close to where the express was wrecked.'

'Yes,' Cardish admitted.

'What was the purpose of that lightning journey?'

'To try and stop the express!'

'But you didn't, Mr. Cardish! Why not?'

'Because the car got a burst tyre. You can question the driver — he'll tell you quickly enough!'

'The Leicester police have already made that inquiry at our request. You are correct in stating the car had a puncture. The driver apparently had difficulty in fixing the spare wheel and told you it would take him about half an hour. You didn't stay and assist him. You left him and returned in about forty-five minutes. He was waiting for you in the car.'

'That's right, he was.'

'And where were you in the forty-five minutes?'

Cardish was silent, trying to keep up with the machine-gun rapidity of the inspector's questions.

'I'll refresh your memory,' Vincent said dryly. 'You headed for the nearest signal box, situated on the main Crewe-London line. Before you reached it you apparently changed your mind and instead followed the railway line for a while.'

'I did, yes,' Cardish admitted tautly. 'I had decided to try and set the signals at danger. There was a set of signals about a mile distant.'

'Before those signals were reached, Mr. Cardish, the smash occurred, not very far from the spot where you must have been.'

'Yes.'

Vincent sat back a little in his chair, pondering. 'You were seen by the man in the signal box — the box you at first had decided to approach. He noticed you had in your hand an odd type of weapon, or gun, or something — '

'At that distance he couldn't have noticed any such thing!' Cardish snapped.

'He could — and did — with field glasses. His box is a lonely one, as you know, and it is his custom to study any unauthorised person beforehand through his field glasses. If he doesn't like the look of them he telephones immediately to the nearest station — which was what he did in your case. He distinctly saw you with the instrument, or whatever it was, in your hand.'

'Then?' Cardish waited in tight-lipped silence.

'I have told you what happened then. You changed your mind, went up the line, and the crash followed.'

'And from all this circumstantial evidence you arrive at the preposterous conclusion that I wrecked the express?'

'Men have done even worse things to keep themselves in public favour.'

'The whole thing's a lot of rubbish — '

'Do you admit that you have this instrument which the signalman saw?'

'Certainly I have it.'

'Licensed?'

'It does not require a licence.'

'Then what kind of an instrument is it? I would like to see it.'

Cardish got to his feet. 'No doubt you would, inspector, but I don't intend to permit you. What is more, I think you are greatly exceeding your authority and I am not answering any more questions.'

'For my part,' Vincent said, also rising, 'I am trying to give you a chance to explain matters. Since you seem unwilling to do so I have nothing further to do than charge you with complicity in connection with the express disaster and ask you to come along with me.'

'I'll be damned if I will! Where's your authority?'

The inspector held out the warrant and the detective-sergeant rose up beside him.

'Very well,' Cardish said quietly. 'But believe me, the law could not be further up a gum tree than on this occasion!'

6

In the beginning Cardish was entirely confident that he could wriggle out of the unpleasant tangle in which he found himself, and he engaged the best possible counsel for the purpose — but the counsel was not a magician and there were many damning points.

Relentlessly cross-examined, Cardish found himself on one foot most of the time.

'What,' demanded the prosecuting counsel, 'was in your mind when you headed towards that signal box?'

'I was intending to destroy the signalman's memory of his occupation and take over myself, stopping the train.'

The counsel was plainly shaken, but he kept control of himself.

'You intended to destroy the signalman's *memory*? How? Be explicit!'

'That is rather difficult. That weapon can locally destroy a portion of memory.'

There was an incredulous murmur in the crowded courtroom. Cardish hesitated, remained silent, and then the prosecuting counsel looked at the acid-faced judge.

'M'lud, I would mention that the weapon concerned has been examined by various scientific experts and none of them can definitely state its precise purpose. If it has any purpose at all it is probably used after the fashion of an acetylene welder — though even this is open to doubt, as none of the experts has been able to make the instrument operate.'

'None of them ever will,' Cardish said coldly. 'I'm the only one who knows how to operate it, and I am keeping that secret to myself. The fact remains it *does* produce a local amnesia.'

'In which case.' the judge observed, 'it is a highly dangerous weapon to possess. And I would remind the prisoner that he is not helping his case any by withholding information in this fashion.'

'Sorry, m'lud.' Cardish apologised. 'I refuse to explain.'

'Why?' snapped the counsel. And as Cardish merely shrugged, 'I'll tell you why! Because actually that instrument is a new-fangled type of oxy-acetylene welder, capable of destroying steel at high speed. I suggest you deliberately melted a portion of the railway line which — '

'I protest, m'lud!' Cardish's counsel exclaimed, rising in anger.

'You will have ample opportunity to register your protest — as well as exercise your undoubted legal skill — at the proper time, Sir Arthur. Proceed, Mr. Halshaw'

The prosecuting counsel returned to the attack, and he kept it up with relentless force. Why the decision to ignore the signalman after all? Because there was not time. Why the trip down the railway line? To set the signals at danger. And there was not time for this, either? No . . . Back and forth, up and down. The prosecuting counsel did not miss a single trick, and every time he kept coming back to the mystery instrument about which Cardish refused to speak. By the time the cross-examination was over

Cardish felt about ready to drop.

'Is it true,' the prosecuting counsel demanded, abruptly changing his tactics, 'that you can see the future Mr. Cardish?'

'Perfectly true.'

'And how did you acquire this — er — beneficial gift?'

'I was struck by lightning during the great Lakeland storm this summer.'

'I see. Now, you have said that you foresaw this railway accident and tried to stop it. I have proved by various expedients that you could have caused the accident in order to make it come true; but let us take another aspect of the matter. If you can foretell one event you can presumably foretell another.'

'I can, yes.' Cardish wondered vaguely what was coming next.

'Well, then, let us take a simple thing.' The counsel looked at the clock. 'Something provable within the next five minutes. I am aware, m'lud, that this is without precedent,' he apologised, with a humble glance towards his lordship, 'but I ask your indulgence to prove a point.'

'You may proceed, Mr. Halshaw.'

'I thank you, m'lud. Now, Mr. Cardish, it is exactly half-past three. You can foretell the future accurately, you say. Very well, then, where will I be in five minutes? What will be my position in this courtroom? And remember I shall do all in my personal power to disprove your forecast.'

Cardish smiled wearily. No Mazorian telescope could help in this. He could not identify people, nor could he see inside buildings. And he could only see 24 hours ahead anyway.

'I am not going to use a superb gift so that you may try and put it to ridicule,' he retorted. 'I'll have nothing to do with the challenge!'

'Which is no more than I expected,' the prosecuting counsel sneered. 'Asked point-blank to prove your powers you carefully avoid doing so. I leave it to the jury to draw their own conclusions from that!'

Upon which he abruptly ended his onslaught and Cardish's own counsel took over. It was no use, though.

The ground had been cut from under

his feet right at the commencement, and despite all his legal tricks he and Cardish could both feel that the battle was lost.

How much lost was shown three hours later when the jury brought in a verdict of 'Guilty', which pinned Cardish down as the main instigator of the railway smash. It was not a murder charge as such, but most certainly manslaughter — and that same evening the papers carried the sensational headlines:

VOLTA FOUND GUILTY!
SEER GETS 15 YEARS!
TRAIN WRECKER EXPOSED!

The details were endless and lurid. Few cases had excited such public interest, and there were indeed many thousands who immediately started to band together to get up a petition, not so much because they though Cardish had had a raw deal, but because they saw his clairvoyant wizardry in jeopardy as far as they were concerned.

The radio and TV also took the matter up and did the very thing that Cardish had striven so far to avoid. His own name was mentioned, and 'Volta' merely referred to as his alias, or business name. The *Daily Flashlight* came out with an acrimonious leader against the workings of the law, and swore it would move heaven and earth to prove that Cardish was innocent and that he really was the seer he claimed to be.

And Cardish himself? Imprisoned, ostracised, he took his fate calmly enough. In some ways he could afford to for he was not as other men. Even though he languished in jail he was also free, wandering the mighty laboratories of Mazor, fully aware of the predicament of his Earth double.

'You brood, Earthman,' the First in Mathematics commented, as he came upon Cardish seated, thinking, before the huge time-telescope. 'Would I be considered too personal if I asked the nature of the trouble?'

'It's something outside your range, sir,' Cardish replied quietly, and at that the Mazorian seemed inwardly amused even though his unemotional face did not alter in expression.

'There are few things beyond our range, Earthman. However, if you do not wish to confide, so be it — '

He turned away to his usual obscure scientific tasks and Cardish went on pondering, trying to devise some way in which he could extract himself from the dilemma on Earth. He was two people, was he not, and yet ruled by the same individual will? On the one side freedom and vast science, and on the other captivity for fifteen years. Surely there must be *something* . . . ?

But apparently there was not. At least not that he could think of then. His thoughts were disturbed finally as the intercom radio equipment signalled for attention, and the First in Mathematics switched it on and listened to the babble of words in his own complicated language. Cardish fancied he heard the word 'Earth' repeated once or twice, and once even there was, he was confident, a reference to his own name . . . He turned to the time-telescope and switched it on, moodily surveying Earth one day hence.

Not that it mattered any more since his Earth self had been abruptly removed from foretelling the future.

Idly, as the First in Mathematics conversed with the speaker at the other end of the radio communication, Cardish wandered the time-telescope over Earth. Then suddenly he gave a start and watched intently. He blinked in astonishment. The instrument was centred directly upon Rio de Janeiro, though not for any specific purpose, and there was something very peculiar happening to that South American city. It was literally falling apart, its buildings disappearing in clouds of dust as enormous fissures gaped in the broad streets.

Then came the people, scurrying and whirling like leaves before a gale, and not seeming very much bigger either. In the space of perhaps four minutes the great city was a crumbling chaos of flame and ruin, the scene of devastation being gradually obscured by smoke and impenetrable dust.

'Earthquake,' Cardish whispered, a gleam coming into his eyes. 'I wonder now — Is this a possible chance?'

'If I might have a moment of your time, Earthman?' It was the voice of the mathematician. 'I regret disturbing what seems to be your only interest — surveying through that telescope — but the present matter is quite urgent.'

'What matter?' Cardish looked up impatiently.

The cold eyes of the Mazorian held him relentlessly, even though that alien face did not alter expression.

'A singular state of affairs appears to have arisen on your world, Earthman. In your country the broadcast reports are making great moment of the fact that one Walter Cardish — the same name as yourself, you will observe — has been foretelling the future and has received imprisonment for some kind of offence.'

'Well?' Cardish asked, his heart beating rapidly. 'How does that concern me? Many Earth people have identical names; and in some cases even the first and second names are duplicated.'

'Very typical of Earthlings' lack of organisation! In this case, however, I do not feel inclined to dismiss the matter as coincidence, any more than did the radio observer who contacted me just now over the intercommunicator. It would appear that this Walter Cardish has been foretelling the future with an amazing accuracy, an accuracy quite impossible indeed unless he has some way of seeing the future and knows he cannot be wrong — '

'Some of us have that gift,' Cardish said, shrugging.

'And have any of you a weapon which causes local amnesia?'

Cardish was silent, feeling oddly chilled.

'Apparently,' the Mazorian continued, walking majestically back and forth as he talked, 'this Earthly Walter Cardish has come into possession of what appears to be one of our own amnesia guns. Earth scientists cannot understand how it operates, but the radio report of court proceedings says that this Walter Cardish *does* know how it works and refuses to explain. He has also said that he intended to *destroy* the memory of a signalman worker. How do you imagine he has in his hands a secret that is ours alone? Why do you imagine his name happens to be identical with yours?'

'I don't know — ' Cardish muttered, lowering his eyes. 'The whole thing's a mystery to me. It must be obvious to so great a scientist as you that I have not the intelligence to transmit thought across dimensions — or even across this laboratory — so I can't explain how my namesake knows so much.'

The Mazorian's silence was bleakly terrifying.

'Further,' Cardish finished, with an obvious desperation, 'no man can be in two places at once, so plainly the Earth Walter Cardish and myself have no connection.'

'The situation,' the mathematician said slowly, 'calls for a great deal of careful thought. There is something here that leads me to believe we may have been greatly mistaken in our judgment of you, Earthman. If that proves to be correct I can assure you that you will bitterly regret your lack of frankness. I will confer with my associates upon this singular matter.'

The Mazorian swung abruptly and left the laboratory. Cardish remained where he was, feeling very sick and very far away from home. The position would have been bad enough if it had had a parallel on Earth; but here, the only Earthman on Mazor, the sensation of loneliness was overwhelming. Yet, with sufficient effort it could be overcome by losing himself within his Earth self . . .

'Earthquake in Rio — tomorrow.' Walter Cardish sat up suddenly on his prison cell bunk and blinked into the gloom. No doubt about that. Commencing at four-thirty tomorrow afternoon! That's the one chance I need!'

To have the chance was one thing but to utilise it was decidedly another. Visitors were not allowed, and in any case the notice was too short. Cardish's first thought was Gascoyne or the editor of the *Flashlight*, but communication with the outside world was not permitted. The only other possibility was his defence counsel whom he was permitted to see if he had something to impart which might still prove his innocence.

Accordingly the lawyer arrived early the following morning at the prison and the interview was permitted.

'I think I may have something.' Cardish insisted, as the legal man listened impartially. 'I was convicted chiefly on the ground that I didn't foretell the future when the prosecution gave me the opportunity. That, and the fact that I engineered the rail smash to make one of my prophecies come true.'

'I must warn you that you are simply going over old ground, Mr. Cardish,' the lawyer sighed. 'You can't get a retrial on those grounds. Don't forget that the instrument about which you refused to speak was also cited as a new-fangled oxyacetylene gun with which you melted part of the railway line — '

'Oh, forget all that!' Cardish waved a hand impatiently. 'How would my chances be if I foretold a tremendous disaster in a foreign country for four-thirty this afternoon? I could hardly fix a thing like that when I'm in this damned jail, could I?'

'Hardly. What is this foreign disaster you speak of?'

'Rio de Janeiro will be partially destroyed by a violent earthquake at four-thirty this afternoon. I *know* it will. I want you to inform the editor of the *Daily Flashlight* and tell him he must contact the South American Government immediately and have people evacuated.'

The lawyer was silent. He knew nothing of Cardish's dual self, and being hidebound by law as well he could be forgiven for looking sceptical.

'I was never more serious about anything in my life,' Cardish insisted. 'The fact that this forecast will come true ought to do much to help me out of this mess.'

'Well, I'll do all I can,' the lawyer promised, rising. 'I will see the editor personally and explain things. I'll also keep in touch with you.'

He picked up his briefcase and departed. Without any great enthusiasm he reported everything to the *Flashlight* editor and that worthy absorbed the facts and did not commit himself in any manner; but the moment the lawyer had gone the editor became a whirlwind of activity, even to the point of getting out a special edition of the *Flashlight* with Volta's warning sprawled in two-inch type across the front page. For the editor it was the springboard from which to launch his threatened attack on the law for its miscarriage of justice.

The B.B.C. took up the cry, glad of a change from the usual stereotyped news bulletins; and the South American Government was also informed. Of itself that Government would probably not have taken action, but the people in the city itself were quite capable of listening to British broadcasts — and many thousands did. It was they who insisted on an evacuation just in case. If no earthquake came it wouldn't make any difference.

For all that, to evacuate completely a city the size of Rio within a few hours is impossible, which was why there were many thousands still left — and which Cardish of Mazor had seen in the time-telescope — when the earthquake came.

The news stunned the world — not only because there had never been so violent a 'quake in South America before but because it had been foreseen to the very hour by the man whom the law had flung into prison as a charlatan! Why this being Volta was superhuman! He must be! And tens of thousands owed their lives to his warning. From afar, in safety, they had seen the city shaken to its depths and its almost total demolition in flame and in-rushing tidal waters. Such a hubbub as there had never been before went echoing round the world, and even the grey impartial justices of Great Britain could not ignore it.

Release the Great Volta! Since he had been correct on this occasion, and indeed on so many thousands of others, there was every possibility he had been correct about the Crewe-London express, but unimaginative officialdom had seized upon a few apparently damning circumstances to put him out of the way.

Release him! The cry to restore freedom to Volta was far louder than the shouts of those who suffered at the hands of his devastating prognostications — the small-time bookies, the weather forecasters, the palmists, the pools promoters . . .

Finally Cardish was released. A form of legislation had to be adopted to do it so the law could save its face. The truth of the matter was the law was scared by the juggernaut power of public opinion and had to submit. So Cardish emerged again to the outer world, his fame tenfold greater by reason of the ordeal he had undergone.

But in the background the law waited. They only wanted him to make one mistake to hurl him straight back into jail again. Not that the law hated Cardish; not indeed that one half the legal men doubted his power to read the future. The real truth was that many were becoming afraid of him. He knew too much, and like most men who know too much it would be better if he were silenced. The big people did not like him, and such is the deplorable state of our society the big people have the power of enforcing their wishes.

Though he was by no means insensible to the 'underground movement' against him Cardish returned to his office and his usual business. The only thing annoying him was that the college to which he had planned to send Tommy had unexpectedly found his admission impossible due to a very full list, so another and less famous seat of learning would have to be used . . .

And on Mazor Walter Cardish was worried. Cardish of Earth knew exactly what Cardish of Mazor was experiencing, but he tried to avoid brooding over it as far as he could . . . And it was not easy, for the First in Mathematics was on the warpath.

'I have conferred with my associates, Earthman,' he said briefly, several 'days' after the release of Cardish from jail, 'and we have come to the inescapable conclusion that by a scientific means which at present eludes us, you have succeeded in maintaining a mental link with a twin brother on your native planet. There can be no other answer. Why you gave the same name as your brother we do not know, but we feel you had an ulterior reason.'

Cardish did not say anything. Inwardly

he was surprised at the twin brother angle. Even yet the mighty minds of Mazor had not grasped the real truth — or else it was that the real truth was so uncommon that it had never occurred to them.

'A mental link between twins is anything but unusual,' the mathematician proceeded. 'We of this planet know how tightly intertwined can be the minds of twins, but that this mental link can exist across different spatial dimensions is an interesting discovery. We had always believed it to be limited to the confines of a single planet. However, the fact remains that to your brother you have transmitted, either willingly or unconsciously, a great deal of valuable information. He has set himself up as a seer. To that we raise no objection; but we do take a serious view of his having the secret of our amnesia gun.'

'Why should you?' Cardish asked, making up his mind to play up the twin brother angle, since that seemed to be the Mazorian's line of action. 'He only uses it to protect himself, same as I use mine for the same purpose.'

'You, Earthman, are on an alien world and watched over by those who could destroy you instantly if you dared use your weapon outside the permitted limits. On your planet it is different. Your twin has a weapon which, in the mass, could wipe out an invading army by destroying the memory of its commanders.'

'Yes, I suppose so.' Cardish agreed slowly, the thought not having occurred to him up to now. 'But — but what invaders could there be? On my planet most of the nations, though they grumble a good deal at each other, are prepared to live peacefully these days.'

'I was thinking,' the Mazorian responded, 'of *inter-dimensional* invaders. Ourselves, for instance.'

Cardish turned sharply to meet the inscrutable eyes. 'You! But I understood that everything here was perfect — that you'd studied Earth for years purely for scientific interest. Why this sudden decision to invade?'

'It has been forced upon us, Earthman, and you are directly responsible! You do not suppose for one moment that we will permit your twin to retain the secret of the amnesia gun, do you? Give him time to hand it over to your Earth manufacturers and thereby create thousands of giant amnesia guns? No! Why, that would make your world invincible, and threaten the success of our planned invasion — '

'*Planned* invasion?' There was shocked surprise in Cardish's voice.

The Mazorian smiled coldly. 'You are a fool, Earthman! Did you really think for one moment that I would reveal to you *all* of our secrets? Our spy satellites, for instance. To you they seemed to represent an amusing toy, but we would never have expended vast scientific resources for the sake of mere scientific curiosity. No, they have a much greater purpose!'

'Which is?' Cardish asked dully.

'We have observed your world at close quarters for many years, and have pin-pointed all of your various military bases and missile defence systems. These can be neutralized right at the start of our invasion. And, apart from telescopic TV cameras, each satellite is equipped with a special transmitter that, when activated, will effectively heterodyne much of your worldwide military radio communications systems, seriously weakening your defensive capabilities.'

'Who the hell are you and your race that you should decide to invade Earth and every living thing upon it?' Cardish demanded, in sudden heat. 'All because of one trifling scientific secret!'

'The secret is *not* trifling, Earthman. It is extremely valuable; far too valuable indeed to be left in one man's hands. We are decided. Before the amnesia gun can be put into production we shall visit Earth and exterminate this twin of yours and take the gun from him — Obviously such a journey with the hazards it entails must also have another purpose to make it worthwhile, so whilst about it we will take over Earth for our own purposes. We have already been planning an invasion of Earth for some time, and had been trying to create a dimensional portal at ground level — which would make our invasion so much easier — '

'And you've failed!' Cardish snapped.

'Your apparatus caused chaos in the Lake District and is clearly too dangerous to use. It only succeeded in bringing me here — and even that was an accident.'

'A very fortunate accident, Earthman.' Again that cold, deadly smile. 'Tell me, why do you think we have permitted you to live amongst us these past weeks?'

'You said . . . ' Cardish paused uncertainly. What *had* the alien said? Cardish flogged his memory. Something about wanting to study his reactions to their world, hadn't it been? A chill struck him as he recalled a later exchange, when the Mazorian had told him about the time-telescope, and had abruptly become evasive. Suddenly things were falling into place . . .

As Cardish remained silent, the alien spoke again.

'The *only* reason you were permitted to live was so that we could study you. All the time you have been here, quite unknown to you, invisible rays have been directed at you, analyzing your bodily energy, and taking readings. Our computers have been analyzing the results. We now know exactly the difference in vibratory energy between Mazor and Earth at ground level.'

'You mean . . . you mean that I have unwittingly aided you in perfecting a dimensional portal?' Cardish said haltingly.

'Not yet. In *time* we would have had the complete answer, but because of your duplicity we shall have to bring forward our departure because there is nothing to prevent this twin of yours being warned by you of our intentions. But we have now learned enough from you to be able to alter our bodily energy — and that of our machines, weapons and transport — enabling us to comfortably exist on your planet at ground level. The only problem is *getting across* to your dimension in the first place. Instead of invading at ground level — which would have been easier — we shall just have to invade your world from space, using the same technology as our satellites.'

'From space?' Cardish was incredulous. 'But how — and why?'

The Mazorian's cold smile was replaced

by a look of irritation. 'Have you no memory of what you have already been told, Earthman? How? By using spaceships, of course, and as to why, have I not previously explained to you that the vibrational barrier between dimensions is much thinner in space away from a planet? We will fly out from here into space, cross into your dimension, and in doing so alter our vibratory levels to correspond to your Earthly dimension. Then — we shall descend to the Earth below!'

'And destroy its peoples?' Cardish asked sickly.

'As to the people of your planet, we shall not destroy them — any more than we need for our own defence; instead, we will use them.'

'You mean make slaves of them?'

The mathematician shrugged. 'They are assets in that they can be made to work and work they shall.'

Cardish was silent. The Mazorian regarded him dispassionately.

'I suppose,' he mused, 'that we could destroy you and so wipe out the link between you and your twin, but that would be no use, for by now you have probably mentally warned your twin of what is coming. No, Earthman, you shall keep your life for the time being. You will be useful in directing us when we reach your planet.'

'You'll not get away with it,' Cardish said bitterly. 'You have mistaken us all along for insects and rabble. We're not, you know. We're a lot cleverer than you think. I'm not a good specimen of my race by any means. In an I.Q. I'd probably rank bottom.'

'I.Q.?' the Mazorian queried.

'Intelligence Quota. Just a saying we have on Earth. Before you take a risk like attacking Earth for the sake of nailing one man I should have a look through this time-telescope of yours and make sure how the battle will go.'

'To see only 24 hours ahead would not be conclusive. No, Earthman, we need no survey of time to know what the answer must be. We have knowledge two thousands years ahead of yours — with that the answer cannot be in doubt — However,' the Mazorian concluded, 'I am glad you mentioned what you fancifully call the 'time-telescope'. It reminds me of something.'

Turning to it he made an adjustment to a knob that looked like a combination lock. Then, smiling acidly, he looked back at Cardish.

'From here on, my friend, your twin will have to make his *own* prognostications,' he explained. 'You have abused the privilege we gave you by handing on secrets and knowledge of future time, therefore the privilege ceases from this moment. You are not our guest any more, Earthman, but our prisoner! This apparatus is now locked and I alone know the combination.'

Cardish stared and without another word the Mazorian left the laboratory — just as the secretary-receptionist in Cardish's office also went into her own domain and left him gazing blankly in front of him.

'Locked it!' he whispered. 'Hell's bells, that's the finish as far as I'm concerned!'

He sat pondering, struggling to realise that in a few seconds of time his amazing 'gift' of reading the future had been wiped out. And, if the First Mathematician of Mazor knew anything about it, the opportunity would never present itself again! It was the sudden, devastating end of the road.

The receptionist appeared again. 'Mr. Haslam is here, sir, for tomorrow's forecast on — '

'I can't see him,' Cardish interrupted, white-faced. 'Shut the main office door. I don't wish to be disturbed.'

'Shut the — ? Oh, very well, sir. Shall Mr. Haslam come back later?'

'I — I don't know. Tell him I'll get in touch with him.'

Puzzled, the redhead retired. Cardish clenched his fists and sat thinking, at the same time sitting as his double in the Mazorian laboratory across the dimensional gulf. At length he rang the bell and once more the redhead came in.

'Yes, sir?'

'Take a seat, Miss Gadshaw, I'm afraid I have a surprise for you. May even be a shock.'

The delectable Miss Gadshaw opened

her mouth a little but did not say anything.

'I have decided,' Cardish said, 'to retire from this profession. I find the strain far too great for me and I'd rather get out of it now whilst I'm reasonably well than wait for a complete mental and physical collapse.'

'Yes, sir,' Miss Gadshaw agreed. 'You mean a vacation?'

'I mean finish, young woman! I owe you your salary until the end of the month, and — here it is.' Cardish scribbled out a cheque and handed it over. 'You know my home address if you should require a reference. I'll be only too pleased to commend your honesty and patience to any new employer.'

'Thank you, Mr. Cardish.' The girl flushed rather warmly. 'I've sort of enjoyed working with you. You're so wonderfully clever the way you see things happening before they do.'

Cardish smiled tautly. 'A Chinese philosopher once said: 'For everything there is a price', and I'm just beginning to see what he meant — Incidentally, Miss

Gadshaw, I have one absolutely reliable forecast to make. Soon the world will have it. As my secretary you might as well know first — Earth will be invaded by aliens from another dimension in a little under a week.'

'By aliens!' Miss Gadshaw's eyes went wide. 'Like they put on the movies, you mean? Winged men and things?'

'These won't be winged, and they won't be play-acting. Take it from me they'll prove the most ruthless, deadly, scientific foes this world has ever known. If you want a final spot of fatherly advice I'd suggest you don't take another job but instead join the women's services. You'll be safer.'

'Th-thanks. I'll think about it anyhow.'

The girl shook the hand Cardish held out and then went slowly out of the office, her face entirely dazed. Cardish waited until he heard the outer office door close behind her and then he hurried through and bolted it. Crossing to the telephone he spoke first to Gascoyne at the Research Institute and then to the editor of the *Flashlight*, securing their respective promises to come over right away for news of exceptional importance.

They arrived within half an hour. Cardish bolted the door after them and led the way into his private office.

'Well?' the editor questioned, eternally a man of action. 'Give! What's all this about, Mr. Cardish? My time is very valuable.'

'I know, my good friend, but you'll think it well spent on this occasion. You can run a headline on this style: 'Aliens to Invade Earth in Seven Days!' And believe me there's no joke about it.'

It was not often the go-ahead editor of the *Flashlight* was caught with his mouth open, but he was this time — just for a moment.

'But that's comic strip stuff!' he protested. 'Dammit, Volta, what are you trying to do?'

'Warn the world!' Cardish snapped. 'Naturally I'm giving you the chance of the exclusive.'

'This absolutely right?' Gascoyne asked quickly, and Cardish nodded.

'Definitely. We've got to move fast too. It's *me* the Mazorians are after, and they don't give a dam' how many people they slaughter in their efforts to locate me.'

'I feel,' said the editor deliberately, his eyes jerking from one man to the other, 'that I have just walked straight into the booby hatch! What in hell are you two talking about? Why should these Maz — er — aliens — want to find *you*. Cardish? For that matter, how do you *know*?'

Cardish hesitated. 'You've been a good friend to me,' he said finally, 'therefore I — '

'Don't get our relationship wrong. Cardish! I'm a news editor and therefore no friend to anybody. I'm out purely for what I can get. I'd blast you as much as praise you if I thought it was good copy.'

'All right, have it your own way.' Cardish smiled tiredly. 'You've taken a lot on trust and I've never told you anything definite — but now you might as well know. *But* it is not for publication. My secret is in the strictest confidence.'

'All right, all right — I promise not to

divulge it. What *is* this secret?'

'I'm a man of two worlds,' Cardish explained. 'I have two bodies and one mind. Or rather one body split into two by an accidental electrical process allied to complicated mathematics. Cutting a long story short I live here and on Mazor — a world in another dimension — simultaneously!'

'And I'm Nero's uncle,' the editor said frankly: at which Gascoyne lost his temper.

'This is no time to be sarcastic just because you don't happen to be a scientist! Cardish is giving you the facts — I know because I've been in on this since the start.'

'But hang it all, man, how can — '

'Listen to the details,' Cardish insisted. 'They're true but you can please yourself whether you believe them or not. I'm merely telling you everything so you can judge how reliable my forecast is. I know you'll have to be dead sure before stampeding the public with an invasion scare.'

'You're darned right I have. All right, let's hear it.'

Cardish gave the details, so thoroughly

it took him half an hour. Gascoyne knew most of the facts, but he looked up intently during the closing statements as he heard for the first time of the 'drying-up' of the futuristic well.

'And that's it.' Cardish spread his hands. 'Now you know why I've been able to see the future, why I've now got to retire, and why the Mazorians are going to head this way.'

The editor had become serious. 'As you said, I'm not a scientist,' he admitted finally, 'but I can certainly smell a story when it's near me. And this is one if ever there was! I believe you, Cardish, even against my better judgment, and I'll keep faith with you — but how I'm going to convince the *Flashlight* owners of the validity of the Mazorian forecast I'll be hanged if I know.'

'Simply tell them the Great Volta says so,' Cardish suggested. 'I have been re-established in public favour after the Rio earthquake so there's no reason why I shouldn't be believed. You can add that I'm retiring from business because of nervous strain occasioned by my prognostications.'

'Right!' The editor seemed to make up his mind and rose to his feet, holding out his hand. 'This is definitely going to be the greatest news-scoop that ever hit the headlines, and I'll be out there batting for you for as long as need be. If you've any more hot news later let me have it right away.'

'Naturally,' Cardish promised. 'But I don't expect any.'

Still vaguely wondering whether or not he ought to have his head examined for giving credence to such a tale, the editor went on his way. After locking the door again Cardish gave Gascoyne a grim glance.

'It's a nasty situation,' the scientist said anxiously. 'Especially for you, my friend! To have the knowledge that a race of super-scientists are after your blood can't be very comforting. What do you propose doing about it?'

'Leading them astray as much as possible,' Cardish shrugged. 'I have the one advantage that they still do not know that I am a dual personality. They believe it to be a case of twins, and therefore do

183

not know that I am as constantly aware of them as I am of you, or anybody else I meet on Earth here — It is plain they intend to bring my other self to Earth so I can direct them to where my twin is. I'll direct them all right — to all the wrong places! They'll never catch up.'

'And if they don't they'll destroy everything in their path until they do. The more you prolong your capture the higher will become the toll of life and suffering — If they are as brilliant as you say they are our most deadly weapons will only be popguns beside theirs.'

'We have the amnesia gun — the First in Mathematics gave me the idea himself that it should be mass-produced. I intend to hand it over to the War Ministry, explain its secret — since I have now nothing to lose by doing so — and have it delivered to all the defence forces in the world.'

'I'll back you,' Gascoyne said seriously, 'to the hilt! And I'll get the rest of my scientific colleagues to do like-wise — Keep in touch. I'll see a scientific conference is called right away to discuss the situation. This business is right out-side ordinary military defence, remember.'

Cardish nodded, shook hands, and saw Gascoyne off the premises. The next move was up to the *Flashlight*, after which things would start to move in real earnest . . .

7

Things certainly did move the moment the news hit the streets — once again in a special edition of the *Flashlight*. To Government representives the bombshell was no surprise since the *Flashlight* editor had warned them in advance — but the general effect on the public was chaotic.

Three-quarters did not believe it. The remaining quarter, formerly loyal to Cardish, wavered. And they wavered because they knew he was going out of business and therefore they were losing the goose that laid the golden eggs.

And, such is human nature, they turned on the man who had provided them with a brief, sure-fire financial paradise.

The *Flashlight* editor did not spare ink, energy or time in his efforts to justify the Great Volta. Invasion from Mazor was definitely coming, and every day made the danger greater. In less than a week a

186

fleet of alien spaceships would fall upon the world, and from them would descend such a scourge of death-dealing fury, humanity would wilt before it. Or so the leader articles poetically put it.

Meantime governments the world over were in consultation with scientific bodies. Was this man Volta to be trusted? After all, he had correctly forecast the South American quake. Or was this one of his wilder feats to gain publicity once more? No, it couldn't be that because he had announced he was retiring, so what use would publicity be? Mmmm, might be something in it, but the matter required a great deal of study.

Great deal of study! And every day bringing disaster nearer. Volta had already said that the Mazorian fleet, numbering some eight hundred spaceships, had left Mazor and was now winging through space. Which was correct. Since he was aboard one of the machines he knew what he was talking about.

But you cannot stampede Governments into action, and most certainly not the British Government. Cardish found himself ordered to attend a Cabinet meeting, and here he was compelled to monotonously recount his 'vision'. But he stolidly withheld his personal secret concerning his dual identities. He knew that the Government would not understand it for one thing, and for another they'd blast the information far and wide and thereafter keep tabs on him, which would automatically lead the avenging Mazorians straight to him.

'But *Mazor*, Mr. Cardish!' the Prime Minister exclaimed, spreading his hands. 'A planet nobody even knew existed before you mentioned it! I hope I am not too old-fashioned in my ideas, but this is going too far.'

'Every moment you delay brings to us the certainty of defeat,' Cardish said. 'I am willing to provide the War Ministry with a weapon which may save us. The weapon so recently misconstrued by the law as a new-fangled acetylene welder. In actual truth it is a memory destroyer, and as such — '

'Yes, yes, quite,' the P.M. agreed, clearing his throat. 'The matter of weapons does not yet enter our calculations, Mr. Cardish — '

'But sir, it should! We have only a few days left! Already the armada is on its way.'

'And how do you know that?' The P.M. smiled indulgently. 'Our most powerful telescopes have not so far revealed this armada, and that is the only possible way by which information could be gained. Or have you — er — 'seen' this amazing fleet by some psychic means?'

'For a man of your high authority you talk like a fool.' Cardish lashed out. 'At the moment the fleet is still in it's own space, so cannot be seen. I'm sick of being humoured by a lot of dolts who treat me like a child having nightmares! Take my weapon, call out every defence we've got, and stand by. Nothing can save us if you don't — and even if you do we have very little guarantee of victory. These Mazorians are completely without pity, magnificently organised, and brilliant scientists.'

To call the Prime Minister a fool is not good policy — as Cardish found out shortly after leaving Downing Street. It was not that the P.M. was vicious — it was simply that he could not credit this wizard-prognosticator with his visions about alien invasions, and desperately though Gascoyne and numberless scientists worked on the P.M., the Cabinet and the War Ministry, nothing could shift them from their hidebound disbelief in things outside their experience.

But there was a deeper significance behind the disbelief in Cardish's warning. The law — and that meant the big men at the top of the profession — was still smarting from the insinuation that they had falsely accused Cardish of charlatanism. Now there seemed to be a chance for revenge, especially with so many people vilifying Cardish because he had decided to retire from business.

Moves were made, the scientists were thrust on one side, and Cardish was nailed down on a charge of spreading gloom and despondency without reasonable cause. This was only the beginning of the fire against him. It burst into flame when the law proclaimed that in asserting the Mazorian fleet was already on its way Cardish had revealed definite signs of insanity. He must be crazy because there was no possible reason for his statement — as far as the 'experts' could see.

He was whipped from his home, where he was trying to find a way round the difficulty, charged by the law, and then handed over to a picked bunch of psychiatrists, whose business it was to poke into everything which decent men and women hold sacrosanct. Hands latched to their coat lapels they averred that Cardish was showing signs of dementia, doubtless caused by the severe strain he had himself mentioned in trying to make his forecasts of the future.

Trying to! Plainly the deliverance of thousands from death in the Rio earthquake had been forgotten.

Cardish did not protest at the probings of these so-called geniuses. He was too tired and dispirited for that; but Gascoyne did, and so did the editor of the *Flashlight*.

Together — a powerful combination of Press and Science — they tried to swing

191

public opinion in Cardish's favour, and possibly they might have managed it but for two factors. One was that most of the other newspapers, voicing the opinion of the Government, were dead against them; and the other was that time simply did not allow.

Cardish was quietly forced out of the public eye into a rest home — or so the papers said. They at least spared him the indignity of stating he had been locked up in a lunatic asylum where he could dream to his heart's content and not bother anybody . . .

On the strength of which the Government breathed more freely and turned to matters of more agreeable flavour. Foreign governments, taking their cue from Britain chiefly because Cardish was an Englishman, also relaxed, thankful they would not have to go through all the complicated procedure necessary in the event of war.

For a couple of days and nights the fool's paradise lasted and Cardish's name had vanished from the newspapers — then came the first flash from Mount

Wilson, where stood the world's mightiest telescope. Strange moving specks had been sighted catching the sunlight, and at a rough estimate they were about 115,000 miles from Earth, roughly half the distance of the Moon.

Specks? Yes, specks! Becoming larger! A later flash report said there were about eight hundred of them ... Eight hundred! Hadn't Cardish said something about eight hundred spaceships?

Flurry smote the governments of the world. The members of the British Government, scattered for the weekend recess, came back hastily to an urgent conference. Reports began to come in from other observatories in the clearer climates confirming to the hilt the first report of Mount Wilson!

In twelve hours there was no longer any doubt about it. The objects in space were disc-shaped spaceships and they were definitely heading towards Earth! Cardish — the Great Volta — had spoken the truth, and the complacent refusal of officialdom to believe him was probably going to cost the world tens of thousands

— if not millions — of its inhabitants.

All that could be done at such desperately short notice was done. Defences were hurried into action stations, all the latest scientific paraphernalia was put in position. All men and women reserves were called up. In every part of the world telescopes — by night — remained tuned on the deeps of space, and every hour brought fresh reports of the nearness of the invaders. And the one weapon that might have given Earthlings a chance of hitting back had been rejected — rejected as a new-fangled acetylene welder! It made Cardish, in his small asylum room with its heavy barred window, smile bitterly.

Not that he had been told anything. He had been, and probably would be, left severely alone. He was a lunatic, and only at given times would he be fed and exercised. He knew everything because he was in the leading spaceship amidst the high-ups of Mazor, and everything that was being given forth over the Earth radio was also being repeated in the spaceships' speakers.

'Apparently,' the First in Mathematics

said, viewing Earth impartially through the gigantic floor-to-ceiling observation window, 'your twin has forecast the invasion, Earthman, and got himself imprisoned for his trouble.'

'Apparently,' Cardish agreed moodily, seated like a child in one of the large softly-sprung chairs and marvelling at the incredible smoothness of these Mazorian space cruisers.

'Would you know where to find him?'

Cardish looked up, hesitating. Around him were the men who would conduct the onslaught on Earth, the men without whose scientific guidance the rest of the Mazorians would be utterly lost.

'I might,' Cardish said guardedly, answering the question.

''Might' implies a doubt, Earthman, and we are only interested in certainty. Can you, or can you not, locate him?'

Cardish made a pretence of concentrating deeply, his finger and thumb pinching the bridge of his nose. After a while he glanced up to behold the inhuman stares of the Mazorians fixed upon him.

'It isn't very easy,' he confessed. 'At the

moment there is a considerable amount of mental disturbance between my twin and myself, no doubt caused by the fears of Earth people at the approach of this fleet. When it calms a little I'll probably be able to contact my twin easily enough.'

'For your sake you had better,' the mathematician said. 'The only reason you are alive is so that you may be useful to us, remember. Once that usefulness passes — '

He turned away with a significant glance and studied the approaching Earth through the immense window.

Cardish looked too, with a definite longing and yet not a little fear. He was returning to his home world, certainly, but only to the midst of carnage and destruction. At all costs he was decided *not* to direct the Mazorians to his other self if he could possibly help it, for once that was done they would cease to be interested in either of the Cardishes — and that would mean oblivion.

And how to hold out indefinitely? This was something that caused Cardish to knit his brows and think furiously.

At this same time, back on Earth, the fat was properly in the fire, since it was obvious to tens of thousands of people that the Great Volta had spoken the truth and that invasion was nearly a fact. Furious, panic-stricken, raging mobs turned upon their governments, ready to lynch the powers-that-be for their short-sighted policy. Some also discovered where Cardish was being detained and made a raid on the asylum. But it was hasty and ill-conceived with the result that it was foredoomed to failure.

With such chaos ruling in practically every country, any attempt at organised defence was out of the question. Indeed, as far as Britain was concerned, the military chiefs had been thrown out of office by the mob, who considered themselves far better able to control the situation than a collection of brass-hats.

Those who knew this was not possible, and who had money, fled by the fastest planes from the crowded, seething cities in the hope that in the wider, outlying regions they would find safety from the invaders. Surely the Mazorians would not waste time attacking plains and agricultural areas? They would be bound to strike at the big cities? That the Mazorians had a plan of attack calculated to destroy everything in their path, town and country alike, until they found the twin of Walter Cardish, was something that, mercifully, was not generally known.

Others, who still had a certain sense of duty, stayed at the defences, those of the highest rank taking command from their ejected superiors. It was surprising how in the space of a few hours, ever since the first warning of the invaders had gone forth, a system of defence was scrambled together, embodying all the latest discoveries in scientific and technical research. It was just as well that the grim-faced defenders, their apparatus tuned to the heavens, did not know that they might as well have tried to stop a volcanic eruption with a candle extinguisher.

The first devastating realization came when Earth's military defences tried to fire guided missiles into space to try and knock out the approaching alien fleet. They found their radio-guidance systems had suddenly gone completely haywire. All contact and control over the missiles was lost. They fell back to Earth, burning up in the atmosphere, and spreading dangerous clouds of radioactivity from their warheads as they vapourised.

The Mazorian's had activated the heterodyning devices on their invisible satellites.

Nothing could stop the fleet reaching the Earth.

Furthermore, the Mazorians already had an accurate idea of what was arranged against them. Cardish had seen for himself the uncanny vibratory instruments, working on a basic radar system, which by an 'echo' system gave back a vibratory outline of every object struck. In this way, by simple analysis, the cold-blooded scientists of Mazor were able to piece together the vibratory picture that outlined a particular piece of apparatus,

The fleet was within a hundred miles of London and coasting down swiftly through the high atmosphere levels, when Cardish found himself questioned again.

'Have you any idea yet, Earthman, as to the whereabouts of your twin?'

'Not yet, but I am extremely hopeful.'

The Mazorian shrugged. 'The sooner you establish the location the better. You may save many lives amongst your fellow Earthlings — '

The Mazorian turned aside to the radio equipment and switched it on, speaking in English — and throughout the world, wherever a loudspeaker was in action, his voice boomed forth.

'Earth people, hear this! We seek one of your number, by name Walter Cardish. Intimate through your radio his present whereabouts and many of you will be spared.'

'But only for slavery!' Cardish shouted into the microphone. 'Take no notice of alien lies! I'm an Earthman and I know what is — '

Dead silence. On Earth strained men and women looked at one another. Aboard the spaceship the First in Mathematics turned slowly and looked at the corner into which Cardish had been hurled by one sweep of a mighty arm.

'You do little to improve your chances, Earthman,' the Mazorian commenced. 'Your people might have listened to reason had you allowed me to finish — '

'Why *should* they?' Cardish demanded, springing up. 'All you are trying to do is lull them into a false sense of security by handing over my twin; then you'll swoop and claim as many of them as you can for slave work. Better for them to be warned and hit back at you!'

The Mazorian gave his icy smile and glanced at his colleagues; then as the vessel swept ever lower towards embattled London the mathematician gave his first orders.

London knew in that moment what invasion by a highly-trained scientific race really meant, and probably the most unnerving aspect of the onslaught was that nothing was visibly coming from the hurtling, disc-like machines milling back and forth over the metropolis.

In the main Operations Room, hundreds of feet underground, harassed technicians gazed at their detector instruments and found them completely dead.

The weapons of any normal invader would instantly have been betrayed on instruments like these — but then a normal invader would not be using neutralising beams with which to block any escape of energy from the weapons of destruction he was using. The Mazorians had no intention of giving a clue as to how many weapons they were using, the nature thereof or the vessel using them. Consequently, with hundreds of machines hurtling with shuttle velocity back and forth over the city the defence was both 'blinded' and incapable of moving fast enough to hit back.

Guided missiles being useless because of the blanketing heterodyning radiation being beamed down from space, death or glory pilots, using the very latest jet-fighters flashed out into the gathering dusk in a scream of challenging fury, but not only could they not keep up with the invading discs, but their weapons were out of range as well All the darting and aerobatics the jet-pilots practised failed to make any impression on the Mazorians, and when the jet-planes became too persistent something invisible was jetted from one of the giant discs and the jet attacker simply ceased to be. No smoke, no fire, no explosion — just instant and silent annihilation.

When this fact became obvious to the taut-faced commanders down on Earth's surface the air attack was called off and instead everything was concentrated on defending the city. A terrific hail of anti-aircraft fire was flung skywards, and though the din of the explosions rocked the metropolis to the depths, no impression was apparently made on the fliers flashing over it.

Instead there was retaliation — so immense and devastating it made the defenders gape in horrified amazement. By the use of invisible electronic forces, using a range far higher than any yet examined by any Earth scientist, the Mazorians succeeded in instantaneously transforming whole blocks of buildings into shimmering blue cubes, in the midst of which running and falling people were transiently visible. Then a blinding flash — but no sound — and nothing would be left but an abysmal crater.

This kind of onslaught was not by any means limited to London. In all the big cities there was similar chaos, and so replete with scientific weapons were the disc-machines it only needed three or four of them to gradually reduce a city and its defences to rubble and destruction. Other machines were busy in the regions beyond the cities, to the horror of the wealthy ones who had fled for sanctuary.

Walter Cardish watched this merciless attack on his world in morose silence, seated constantly at the main observation window of the leader vessel and gazing down on the twisting patterns that denoted the ripping of cities into pieces. He saw the scurrying specks of human beings trying to escape — and failing. And through it all, the First in Mathematics and the high-ups around him, so indispensable to this one-sided massacre, surveyed the onslaught with impartial satisfaction.

After four hours of it the mathematician gave the order to cease fire. Through the world there was an abrupt cessation of the raging hell as the disc-machines flashed skywards and were gone, to join the main formation. Some below even believed the attack was over; that there might be a chance to recover and rebuild.

Until the voice of the mathematician came through on various loudspeakers, those few operating from broadcasting stations still in action.

'Earth people, you have seen what we can do and you will realise that there is nothing you can devise which can stand against us. We are prepared to cease attacking you if you find Walter Cardish and tell us over your radio system where you have put him. For the rest, you will consider yourselves our prisoners. We have need of you.'

The mathematician glanced sharply towards Cardish but this time he made no effort to say anything impromptu into the microphone.

'We will give you fifteen minutes to make your answer,' the Mazorian concluded, and switched off. Then he strolled over to where Cardish was hunched on the window-seat.

'Well, Earthman? I trust you are satisfied that we know how to impose our will?'

'I never doubted that you were.' Cardish gave a sigh. 'But you're making a great mistake, you know. You don't understand the psychology of my race. They'll die fighting before they'll be dictated to. Not only my countrymen, either. You'll find every race on Earth dead set against you after the destruction and terror you've unleashed.'

'More fools they! You are the kingpin in all this, Earthman. The carnage and horror can be stopped this moment — whether or not there is a favourable answer to my ultimatum — if you will state where your twin brother is.'

'I don't know where he is. By this time he's probably been killed, which accounts for my not having made contact with his mind.'

'That,' the Mazorian admitted, brooding, 'is a possibility, I suppose. And if it has come about our purpose is accomplished. We wish to stop him handing on the secret of the amnesia gun — '

'Of all the absurd things!' Cardish cried, leaping up. 'How the hell do you think he could hand on *any* secret with civilisation in ruins around him? You plan to make my people your slaves anyway, so what use is the amnesia gun to anybody now?'

'One can never tell,' the Mazorian said coldly. 'Even if your twin *is* dead the gun must be somewhere, perhaps even on his person. Perhaps it would be more to the point if I told your race to produce Walter Cardish dead or alive so that he may be searched.'

He nodded to himself as he thought this one out and then switched on the radio again. He gave forth the 'rider' to his earlier statement and then broke contact again. Supreme in the knowledge of his own power he was quite sure his demand would be acceded to . . .

In which, as Cardish had warned him, he completely misjudged the temperament of Earth peoples. Already reeling from the fury of the attack which had been made upon them they did not seize at the opportunity for surcease — rather they remembered that Walter Cardish had already been wronged by being disregarded when he had given warning. Hand him over to these barbarians into the bargain? Like hell.

Instead the brief respite was used by the military powers to try and get their sadly depleted forces together again. If it meant extermination in the end, all right. Better to die fighting than walk passively into captivity. Which raised another point. Who had spoken on the radio and cut across the Mazorian's earlier statement? It had sounded very much like the voice of Walter Cardish, the Great Volta. Yet that could not be. He was known to be in the Sunbeam Institution . . .

But he was not there any more. The destruction that had hit London and surrounding environs had also hit the asylum and completely wrecked it. Not all the inmates had been killed, or even hurt, and Cardish was one of the lucky ones. Taking advantage of the confusion and the night he slipped away and was gone.

He hurried over rubble-strewn wildernesses, across still smoking craters, stumbled over dead bodies, and finally turned up more dead than alive in the area designated as military headquarters. Just how he had located it was no mystery. On board the Mazorian leader vessel the instruments had shown clearly where the headquarters were. All Cardish had to do was study them through the eyes of his double and then head for that spot.

Sentries finally brought him to the deep underground Operations Room, and here he was studied in amazement by the men who had taken over the military operations

'Get him a drink and some food,' ordered Commander Horley. 'He's out on his feet — '

Not entirely. After a drink Cardish revived quickly He began to talk whilst an orderly gave first aid to his many superficial cuts and bruises.

'I'm Volta, commander — or maybe you recognise me?'

'I'm afraid I don't recognise you, sir.

The picture of Volta was rarely published.'

'Of course. I'd forgotten. Anyway, take my word for it that I am he — the Prognosticator. They had me tied up in an asylum until this onslaught came, then I seized my chance to get free. I believe I can be of great help to you, even perhaps turn the tide.'

'Oh?' Commander Horley gave a weary smile. 'How sir? By predicting the future? Believe me, it needs no prediction. We are absolutely beaten — unless we hand you over — and that we do not intend to do.'

'I am aware of the ultimatum,' Cardish said, 'and I also rather guessed that you would not hand me over. However, I am not going to predict the future on this occasion because for once I cannot visualise it. What I am going to do is give you the basic outline of various weapons which, even if they don't cripple our foes completely, will certainly give them a run for their money.'

Horley stared in some amazement. 'But, my dear sir, I have never heard you mentioned in the inventive field, so how comes it that — '

'If you read the account of my trial you must know of the amnesia gun.'

'Oh, yes!' Horley looked rather surprised. 'That was what you called it. The law had a different name — '

'Never mind the law! *I'm* telling you this amnesia gun is a tremendous weapon and though I withheld the secret before for personal reasons I'm now prepared to hand it over. Any trained engineer will understand the principle. Find me one and I'll do the rest.'

Commander Horley, a desperate man, did not argue any further. He snapped on the intercom.

'That you, Harris? Horley speaking. Have Ted Cartwright of Electronics come over right away — Yes, very urgent. Okay!'

Horley switched off and added briefly by way of explanation: 'Cartwright is in the Electronics section, and one of our best engineers. He's been growing more grey hairs every minute trying to work out how to defeat these damned aliens.'

'By ordinary means by which I mean our highest scientific standard, we'll *never* defeat them,' Cardish said quietly. 'I have inside information on the Mazorians and I know more or less what they're up to.'

'But dammit, man, how *can* you know?' Horley banged his fist on the desk. 'It just isn't possible!'

'To quote Homer, Commander, there 'are more things in heaven and earth than are dreamt of in your philosophy'. Never mind how I know: I just *do*, that's all. Now there are other weapons, too, of which I have a fair knowledge, though I admit it is not exact. However, once again an expert scientific engineer may be able to put the pieces together.'

'You — you mean Mazorian weapons?' Horley was incredulous, and his staff officers were looking up in surprise from the huge operations map.

'Yes, I mean Mazorian weapons. I have discovered the basis of their most deadly weapon, the one that dissolves brick and steel and flesh with equal certainty. It is in the realm of higher electronics, so doubtless your engineer will understand. If he does, can you produce weapons? Are there armament works still undamaged?'

Horley gave a grim smile. 'Plenty! All

over the world and deep underground. No international barrier about this lot either, Volta. We're all in it, fighting the one foe — '

He paused, and looked up as the lean-faced, grey-headed Ted Cartwright entered. He gave an expectant glance and was immediately introduced.

'Glad to know you, sir,' the engineer smiled, shaking hands. 'If ever a man was wronged by the law, you were.'

'We can forget that,' Cardish said quietly. 'As the commander here will verify, I have information on Mazorian weapons with which we might be able to hit back if we can hold out long enough to manufacture the stuff. First, take a look at this design — '

Cardish drew a sheet of paper towards him and began to draw rapidly. His work was plainly not that of an experienced draughtsman but it was nonetheless clear enough for the engineer to follow.

'Mmm, a mighty clever idea,' he said in admiration. 'A cheap diamond point which when exploded generates a vibratory beam directly acting on the area of

213

the brain responsible for memory. Because the charge is weak only the upper cells are affected, thereby destroying only local and not general memory.'

'Permanently.' Cardish added. 'Make guns like this on a giant scale and the Mazorians won't even remember what they're fighting for. Get them in that demoralised condition and then blast them with this — '

He drew more paper to him and started once again to draw, pausing as there presently came through the loud-speaker the voice of the First of Mathematics. He had been expecting it for, aboard the Mazorian leader vessel, he had been watching the alien switch on.

'Earth people, you have been granted extra time to make your answer to my proposal, namely, produce Walter Cardish, dead or alive. Since you see fit to ignore us you have only yourselves to blame for the destruction that is about to descend upon you. Remember, you can halt it at any moment by announcing where Walter Cardish is to be found!'

'I get it!' Horley exclaimed, snapping

his fingers as the voice died away. 'At some time or other, Volta, you have been working as an agent against the Mazorians. Maybe you know more of the Mazorian weapons than they like? Which is why they're wanting you!'

'Could be,' Cardish murmured, working swiftly with his pencil — and by slow degrees, accompanied by a good deal of hard thought, he began to build up the basic power plant of the Mazorian's most deadly weapon.

It was quite the hardest job Cardish had ever undertaken. From long unnoticed study aboard the space machine, both during the journey from Mazor and more recently now the fleet was in action, he had had the opportunity to study how the electronic weapon worked, chiefly because the power plant itself was not shielded in any way.

The reason for this was so that in the event of a breakdown when the moment counted, the fault could be quickly located and rectified. Laid bare, then, was the basis of the Mazorian electronic annihilator — and because they believed

Cardish was not brainy enough to understand it, and also because they believed he had lost touch with his twin, they made no attempt to keep the weapon shielded.

For that matter Cardish did not understand it, for he was no scientist. But then a layman can describe a radio set in detail without understanding it and have an engineer clearly understand what he is talking about. So it was here, the electronic expert asking questions about this or that point and Cardish explaining minutely, which he could easily do by lounging across the Mazorian control room and studying the weapon's innards with apparent detachment.

Far above the underground Operations Room the attack from the discs was resumed, but so far safely hidden from it Cardish went on explaining and the engineer made copious notes. It turned out to be a four-hour session, but at the end of it the electronic engineer's eyes were bright with purpose.

'I get the principle!' he cried. 'I absolutely get it! It is simply a higher order of electronics than we are used to and one that we have therefore never explored. There is no reason whatever why we shouldn't build a weapon like this! Not one, but hundreds, thousands, and then give these super-scientific lice something to think about!'

'You really think that?' Horley questioned eagerly.

'I'm convinced of it! There's just one thing: what happened to that original amnesia gun you had? Didn't the law give it back to you when you were released after the railway smash business?'

'Yes; and having no use for it, and also having a presentiment of danger, I deliberately threw it out of alignment. If anybody has discovered it they'll certainly never 'un-scramble' it — But that doesn't signify. Go to work on these weapons as fast as you can and we'll beat these damned Mazorians yet! They'll never expect to have their own weapons turned against them.'

Cartwright nodded, wasted no time, and hurried out to his own quarters with the sketches to make the necessary contacts with armaments firms the world over. Cardish relaxed a little, smiling faintly in satisfaction.

'Your safest place,' the Commander told him, 'is down here with us. If you go above again you'll either be blasted to bits or else seized by some of the more extreme members of the public and offered to the aliens.'

Cardish nodded. 'I intend to stay here, Commander, and thank you for the privilege.'

'I'm wondering about something. These headquarters are supposed to be a secret. Nobody but those engaged here know the situation. How the devil did you find us?'

'By the same means that I once read the future — Forget it, Commander. This is not the time for irrelevant issues.'

Horley nodded brief agreement and turned his attention to the operations map. By watching the various lights flashing and winking from various parts of the world Cardish was more or less able to read what was happening. Cities were expiring under the electronic waves of the Mazorians, and as they expired their contact lights went out. And in the Mazorian leader ship Cardish also had another view of the battered Earth through the observation window. He remained tight-lipped and silent, waiting through his other self for news of the turning of the tide.

The moves made by the Earth armament chiefs were swift and precise, guided by the indefatigable Cartwright. There was no gainsaying that everything would have gone well, and the tide could probably have been turned, except for one thing.

The over-zealous Cartwright handed on his belief of victory to the ever-present news hawks, and they in turn passed it on to the avid broadcasting companies. In consequence, no more than two hours after he had given all the details, Cardish was shocked to hear — through both his selves — all the facts being given by the radio and TV announcers.

'Through some process which it is not our business to question,' the London announcer said, 'the great Volta has given to us brilliant scientific inventions with which we are confident we can destroy these damnable invaders. If not that, then we can at least hit back with paralysing force. In the field of higher electronics we have the answer to the destruction which has been raining upon us — Stand by, please, for more news as it comes in.'

Within the Operations Room Cardish leapt to his feet in fury. He had been half asleep, but the announcement had blasted him into full wakefulness.

'What the devil's the meaning of that radio announcement?' he demanded, and Commander Horley, yawning over the maps, looked up in surprise.

'Meaning? I don't understand. The public have to have *something* to keep them stimulated — '

'Be damned to the public! It's the Mazorians I'm thinking of! They'll have heard every word of that broadcast and will know what we're doing. Our initiative's lost — completely. And they'll also know that I'm still alive.'

'I don't see,' Horley replied uneasily, 'how we are to stop the news leaking out. It never occurred to me that the

Mazorians would hear us.'

Cardish took no more notice of him. He was living through his other self and looking at the inscrutable faces of the Mazorians grouped around him. Every one of them was gazing frigidly, the high lighting shining on their bald domes. The radio broadcast picked up from Earth had just finished.

'At least you are a man of courage, Earthman,' the First in Mathematics said. 'We will grant you that. Obviously you have passed on the knowledge of our weapons to your twin, which means you knew from the start that he was still alive — and his whereabouts.'

'I don't know his whereabouts,' Cardish lied. 'Nor did I know he was alive. As for picking up information from your machines, how can I help it when I'm amidst them constantly — I begin to think that the real truth is that my twin is picking up information from *me*. I'm not giving it to him deliberately.'

'That is as it may be,' the Mazorian responded briefly. 'The fact remains that you have given your race a very powerful means of defence, but it will not be possible for them to get the various weapons completed before some little time has passed. Now we know their intentions it is our task to see that their plans do not mature. We will unleash upon your home country of Britain and its capital city the full weight of our armament — much of which is on the other machines and therefore outside your prying investigations.'

There was nothing Cardish could do. Sick at heart he heard the mathematician giving his orders to the fleet . . . Yes, there was *one* thing Cardish could do, and he did it. That was to warn those in the Operations Room to get out quick before the deluge of Mazorian destruction descended.

Horley was reluctant to agree.

'My job is down here directing the defence,' he insisted. 'We're safe enough. There's nearly a hundred feet of rock over our heads.'

'I don't care if there's five hundred. I've just had one of my glimpses of the future and I'm telling you in all seriousness that the Mazorians will fling everything they've got at these headquarters — and soon. Weapons will be used which will make the carnage so far seem as nothing by comparison.'

Finally Horley agreed, chiefly because the rest of his staff had firm faith in Cardish's conviction. It was as well they had, for not twenty minutes after they had sought the underground passages that led from the Operations Room hell itself blasted from the invaders.

What inconceivable power it was they used even Cardish did not know, chiefly because the destruction was rained from the fleet proper and not the leader vessel. It was some kind of ray, visible this time, which stabbed with eye-searing brilliance through the night and cleaved through everything it touched. The hundred feet of rock that Horley had imagined so complete a safeguard melted like butter under a griddle as that unholy radiance bit deeper and deeper into the Earth, ripping apart the atoms of matter.

With the destruction of the Operations Room complete the Earth defences, in

Britain anyway, were completely at sea. Nobody was giving orders, so those at the guns could only fire where they saw the enemy and leave it at that. Meanwhile, other searing rays were at work, seeking out the buried armament works and volatilising them wherever they lay. The detectors revealed them because they — the factories — generated a considerable amount of electrical energy. Once pinpointed nothing could save them from devastating annihilation.

Right through the night of horror the devastation continued, the Mazorians using their secret weapon everywhere. By the time the dawn had come the First in Mathematics, sleepless and intent amongst his likewise alert colleagues, gave the order for the ray to be stopped. More than this. he brought the attack to a halt.

'I fancy,' he remarked, glancing at his colleagues, 'that we have little more to worry about concerning these fools of Earth people. Their armament foundries are destroyed and their defences irreparably smashed. It is time we descended and let them know our intentions.'

Cardish, seated in a corner, his hands dangling limply between his knees, did not make any comment. Certainly he did not tell the egotistical Mazorians that not every factory on the face of the Earth had been wiped out. Some, according to news sent by word of mouth — which communication the Mazorians could not hear — were still working at top pressure on the secret weapons. If somehow they could get only a few hundred of them into action they might spring a surprise which would catch the supermen of the alien planet on the hop . . . Best of all would be the annihilation of the master-minds who were back of this whole campaign. If *they* could be killed, the rest of the Mazorians might be overthrown through lack of directives from the supreme authority.

This thought took possession of Cardish. He looked under his eyes at the pitiless beings who had already destroyed a world and were willing to direct operations in the enslavement of tens of thousands of helpless men, women and children . . . The cynical, egotistical First in Mathematics, head of them all, the First in Biology; the First in Physics; and the First in Electronics. These four men were the ones who bore full responsibility for what would happen next, as much as for what had already happened. Yes, with them out of the way . . .

'Your own future, Earthman, is precarious to say the least of it,' the First in Mathematics said, turning. 'We shall descend to this planet of yours and you will then direct us to your twin.'

Cardish shrugged. 'That is impossible. I still have no idea where he is. He was in the Operations Room, but he escaped with the staff into the underworld. I've lost touch again.'

'For your own safety, it would be as well if you found ways and means of regaining contact as quickly as possible.' Cardish became silent, wondering what he must do next. It was quite plain that this business had to end soon, and if at all possible it must end in victory for the Earthlings . . . That one thought dominated Cardish's mind: there was a chance of survival if these four dominating figures could be obliterated.

Cardish was still lost in speculations as the machine made its final dive to Earth and finally landed in the rubble and dust of what had been London. That there was not a soul in sight was hardly surprising. Those who had not fled underground had been decimated — the answer was as simple as that. What fighters and workers there were left, were tucked away in holes and corners, waiting for the one opportunity of receiving amnesia guns and annihilators straight from the production line.

As the airlock was opened and the Mazorians stood surveying the ruin and desolation they had brought about, Cardish found his mind straying to his other self. He was still deep in the underworld, with Horley and the other staff experts, all of them biding their time as well as possible until news should be received that weapons were on their way. By means of radio they were aware that the first Mazorian craft had landed.

'Which doesn't bode too well for us,' Horley commented with a grim glance.

'What are the prospects, Volta? Any more glimpses of the future?'

'Not yet,' Cardish answered quietly, and fell back into thought again. With the other men he was within a huge natural cavern wherein were endless stores and supplies — a great underground arsenal linked by a network of tunnels to what had once been the Operations Room and which had escaped the relentless power of the Mazorians' deadly ray. For nearly half an hour Cardish sat almost motionless, turning over a plan in his mind, and at intervals, thinking of Bertha and Tommy who had presumably gone forever. Not that they were important in his scheme of things. They never had been, indeed, and besides the notion now taking place in his mind was something infinitely greater than an affair of personal ties.

'There's no doubt,' he said finally, as Horley glanced at him, 'that with the four leaders of the Mazorian invasion dead we could probably turn the tide. For that reason I feel it incumbent upon *me* to destroy those leaders.'

'How?' Horley asked dryly. 'I get the

impression that they are far too danger-ous to deal with. Have sense, Volta. You'd never get within miles of them.'

'I believe I would. Don't forget that they want to see me. I should probably have done this much earlier and saved a good deal of carnage — only I didn't know then what I know now. A certain scientific fact.'

'Oh?' Horley waited for an explanation but he did not get one. Instead Cardish took a sheet of paper from the nearby scrap pile and began to write in his precise hand.

When he had finished he read the note through, nodded to himself, and then sealed it in an envelope.

'This,' he said, handing it to Horley, 'is to be read if I do not return here within twenty-four hours. If I do return, which candidly I do not expect to do, you will hand it back. Understood?'

The commander nodded. 'You mean, then, to try and do a deal with these Mazorians?'

'I do. I think there is a way to deal with them. Thanks for the sanctuary you've given me so far — and now I'm on my way.'

Horley shook hands, his rugged face dubious, and with a nod of farewell to the rest of the men Cardish left the big cavern, following the main tunnel which would eventually bring him to the surface. All the time he walked he was thinking of his other self and viewing the Mazorian spaceship's interior through his eyes. And presently, the First in Mathematics turned from his survey of the desolated world and pinned Cardish with his merciless eyes.

'Well, Earthman, have you yet contacted your twin? We do not see that there is anything to stop you, for we remain convinced that he is *not dead*. If, for some reason best known to yourself, you continue in your obstructive tactics, we'll have no alternative but to wipe you out and search for your twin ourselves. Remember that for the betrayal of our secrets you merit death — and will receive it if you fail to — '

'I believe,' Cardish said slowly, 'I know where my twin is, but this is the first intimation. Allow me a moment to try and place the position where he is.'

The Mazorians complied, waiting in stony silence. Then presently Cardish gave a nod.

'Yes, he's no more than two miles from here and I think — though I'm not certain — that it is in his mind to give himself up. Apparently he has only just heard that that is your wish and hopes to stop further massacre by his action.'

The Mazorians looked at one another with derisive smiles. Cardish watched their faces but kept his voice calmly level.

'If you wish, I can direct you to him, and with all respect I submit that each one of you should come so you can be individually satisfied.'

The First in Mathematics glanced at his counterpart in Electronics. 'This may be a trick. Have we adequate protection should we be attacked on leaving the protection of our ship?'

The First in Electronics smiled complacently, fingering the belt of glittering instruments about his waist.

'My detectors will reveal the presence

of any weapons or chemical explosives within a ten mile radius. Once any such objects are detected, a neutralizing radiation can be sent out to disable them.'

'Very well,' the mathematician agreed briefly. 'There is nothing we can lose by so doing. Let us be on our way.'

Without further hesitation he stepped outside into the dusty waste, his three companions following him. Cardish followed them, a small, somewhat bowed figure amidst the majestic all-conquering quartet. Indeed Cardish had every reason to look bowed, for if the scientific fact on which he was basing this last throw of the dice proved to be correct, he was making his final walk this side of eternity.

For two miles the walk persisted, with never a sight of a single soul anywhere, though across the sky there did occasionally streak a distant jet plane, which testified that humanity still lived, though hidden.

'How soon do you expect we shall meet your twin?' the First in Mathematics asked abruptly, as the march continued. 'This primitive method of locomotion, walking, is tiring to beings of our stature.'

For answer Cardish pointed ahead, and at the same time he stopped, filled with an immense and well-nigh intolerable mental confusion. He was now standing in a distant rise of ground alone, and he was also with the Mazorians. Through two sets of eyes he was, for the first time, looking at himself. The mental reaction produced was shattering, though the physical effect was much the same as looking into a far distant mirror.

'He is not bearing any weapons,' the First in Electronics said, consulting his instruments. 'He presents no threat to us.'

'Good,' the First in Mathematics said, and then nudged Cardish with the wicked-looking handgun he had drawn upon sighting the distant figure. 'You go ahead. 'We will follow you. We wish to study you both carefully. There never was such an amazing resemblance.'

Cardish obeyed, a taut little smile about his lips. With every step he took he could hear the Mazorians coming up behind him, which was just as he wanted it. The four of them! The leaders! Without whom the Mazorian attackers would have no guidance; without whom Earth had a chance to live again.

Cardish still went on, half-closing his eyes against the uncanny sensation of viewing himself from two directions simultaneously. Once he nearly stumbled. By a tremendous effort he went on again, at the same time bringing his double down the slope. The Mazorians, advancing majestically, saw the two men extend hands towards each other in the usual Earth greeting. The hands gripped — and for two miles round the area there was nothing but expanding gases, terrific heat, and a concussion that was felt halfway round the Earth. When the confusion had cleared there was no sign of the Mazorians no sign of two Walter Cardishes — nothing except one more smoking crater amidst the general ruin.

*　　*　　*

It was three months later when the last Mazorians were driven from the face of the Earth by the mighty rally attempted by the Earthlings. With what few weapons they had, albeit stolen by Walter Cardish, they hit back with all their power and scattered the demoralized, leaderless hordes — presumably back into space and then to their own dimension.

It was when the vanquishing was complete that it dawned on Commander Horley, chief of the armed forces, that Walter Cardish was the man whose memory should be honoured for the thing which had come about. He had promised to destroy the four Mazorian leaders and apparently had. But how?

Horley remembered the letter Cardish had given him. In the presence of scientists and new political leaders he read it aloud:

'I, Walter Cardish of Earth, know that I am about to die. I am also Walter Cardish of Mazor, and the motivating mind behind both entities. I am not a scientist, but I can remember one basic fact. Two bodies cannot occupy the same space at the same time. If they try to there must be infinite expansion and explosion. That, I believe, is what will happen if I attempt to seize hold of my other self . . . But that is what I intend to do, in the belief it will destroy the Mazorians whom I hope will be accompanying me. If so, destruction will be complete. They do not know the two Cardishes are the same man, otherwise they would be wary. The same yes, but distinct, because the separation of the two entities by electrical and mathematical forces can never put them together again. It's Humpty-Dumpty all over again.

WALTER CARDISH.

'And how right he was,' Horley muttered, looking at the gathering around him. 'And what an incredible fate it was that overtook him.'

Nobody commented immediately, though each was thinking of one outstanding fact — to save the world Cardish had deliberately blown himself and his shadow to pieces.

We do hope that you have enjoyed reading this large print book.

Did you know that all of our titles are available for purchase?

We publish a wide range of high quality large print books including:

Romances, Mysteries, Classics
General Fiction
Non Fiction and Westerns

Special interest titles available in large print are:

The Little Oxford Dictionary
Music Book, Song Book
Hymn Book, Service Book

Also available from us courtesy of Oxford University Press:

Young Readers' Dictionary
(large print edition)
Young Readers' Thesaurus
(large print edition)

For further information or a free brochure, please contact us at:

Ulverscroft Large Print Books Ltd.,
The Green, Bradgate Road, Anstey,
Leicester, LE7 7FU, England.
Tel: (00 44) **0116 236 4325**
Fax: (00 44) **0116 234 0205**

To escape war, humanity takes a drug that kills emotion. But insurgents, including the returning astronauts from a mission to Mars, refuse to take the drug and wage an armed rebellion. The Freedom Army, which includes the Physicist Burges, is beseiged in a bunker. However, Burges constructs a gateway to another dimension — an alternate existence — and ex space pilot Lanson leads their escape . . . only to face an alternate world where humanity is enslaved by a toad-like alien race, the Zytlen!

THE SPIKED BOY

John Russell Fearn

Dick Palmer and Will Snell are great friends, both former highwaymen who were subsequently exonerated. However, they become fugitives from the law again when members of a mysterious gang of murderers and kidnappers use their names to frame them. Then when the gang kidnap Palmer's wife the two friends are plunged into a deadly struggle to rescue her. But they are up against an evil and secret organization — and the sadistic Simon Pendexter, who swings a 'spiked boy' . . .

...PTY

J. F. Straker

On a lonely island in a Scottish loch, Donald Grant and his self-willed wife Kay are staying with his aunt and uncle, and their daughter Janet. Three desperate men, looking for a hideout, have also come to the island: Bull, Fred and Joe, are gunmen on the run from a robbery, and filled with seething mistrust for one another. Now the island community faces fear and violence in a situation that will lead to tragedy . . .